ANA MICHELLE

LONG LIVE THE KING

This book was definitely a team effort, so I want to dedicate this book to my Aunt Beth and my Grandma Sherri who both helped me grind this one out to the very end.

Contents

Prologue

Alaric

I leaned against the pillows that overflowed Raylene's bed, my head tilted back to rest against the wall and eyes closed as I held her in my lap. I heard the door burst open and my head jerked up, eyes flying open. Cora was in the doorway with Cal and Melody on either side of her, each face filled with panic, "Sir, the knife that was used on the queen," Cora's voice was breathless, "the tip is broken."

"What do you mean?" I demanded, feeling the blood in my veins go cold.

"That for the last hour the gold tip has been traveling toward her heart, I don't think we can save her."

"But the herbs." I insisted desperately.

"It would be too big a piece of gold for the herbs to affect. We would have had to physically remove it before sealing in the herbs."

"You mean she's dying?" My world crumbled around me at the question. I wanted to fall to my knees and beg the shifter in front of me to tell me they could save her, that they could save me. I ran a hand through her sweat-dampened hair and my vision blurred as she nodded sadly. I felt Raylene go still in my arms a moment before a soft sigh reached my ears. I looked down and heard her heart stutter to a stop. I felt my throat vibrate moments before the wolf's howl fell from my lips. Curling over her I clutched her to my chest. I felt hollow inside, my heart had shattered when hers stopped.

"Ric?" My name reached my ears and I could hear the questioning pain that matched my own. I looked up through my tears to see Melody in the doorway, Cal behind her, a supportive hand on her shoulder.

"She's gone" the words were no more than a whisper when I could finally get them out.

"The pack is gathered down in the entryway," Cal said, voice filled with sorrow as he pulled his sobbing mate into his chest. I stood, legs trembling, and laid Ray's still form on the bed. I pressed a kiss to her still warm forehead, a goodbye and an apology wrapped into one. I brushed away the falling tears and walked from the room, closing the door behind me. I looked out over the mix of my people and hers, many of whom already had tear-stained faces that were tilted up to me.

"The Queen is dead," I barely felt the hard floor when my knees connected with it.

I was numb as the words rang back to me, "Long Live the King."

Chapter 1

Alaric

I sat in the old worn executive style chair at the old oak desk where I spent so many afternoons with Raylene and my heart ached for her still. It had been a year since her death and the darkness that it had left over the pack was still lingering like wildfire smoke coating the aura of our pack. While I still maintained my mobile home trailer that I moved into when I changed and the repair shop I own back in Bedal, I haven't been to either of them in several months as the memories there tend to suffocate me. I couldn't bring myself to sell the trailer, even though I couldn't stay there in the place where I claimed Raylene as mine just last year. Since her death a year ago I had taken up permanent residency in the clan home, her home. I was doing my best to find a balance between our two people, her clan of purebreds and my pack of attack survivors, none of them would ever be victims.

The divide that had nearly destroyed us all was slowly beginning to close, but the distrust that Anabella and Marco had created in the pack and had eventually led to Ray's death was still there. I ended up letting a few members of the pack handle Marco after her death. I'd never wanted to lay eyes on him again after what he had done to my mate, and I was afraid that I would have lost control of the beast inside of me at the sight of him. In the first few days controlling my beast, the beast that Raylene helped me to realize was only a part of me and not all of who I was, had been a struggle of its own. I had left Annabella in the cells until after Raylene's funeral, she was just another of my people I was unable to face.

When I finally felt I had enough control of myself I went to the basement and released her. She had thrown herself at me crying and begging me to reconsider when I told her she was banned from the pack and would have to flee immediately. I walked away as she fell to her knees, groveling for forgiveness, something I was unable to even consider. Alana and Tanya had taken Annabella to her home and helped her pack her belongings before the pack lawyer had her sign the home over to Avianna, her younger sister. I allowed them to help her relocate to another pack in Portland. Close enough that she could still have a relationship with her sister, but far enough away that I would never have to lay eyes on her again. After the first month Avianna had begun to go see her every other weekend. The relief in her eyes when I told her that I was ok with it made me hurt for her, and soon she was making the trip almost every week. When her visits came to a near stop I didn't ask questions. I knew the shy Omega shifter would come to me if and when she felt she needed to, until then I would leave her to her mate.

I looked up when there was a soft knock on the office door. I had to force a smile on my face when I saw Melody standing in the doorway with her chubby baby on her hip. "Hey," her voice was soft, bordering on motherly.

"How are you doing Mel?" I stood from the chair and made my way over to them. There was no way I would have been able to make it without these two and Cal, Melody's mate, moving into the mansion with me.

"We are fine, but we are wondering how Uncle Ric is doing." I smiled down and gave the Omega a side hug before kissing the dark curly hair that was starting to cover the tiny head more and more every week. Melody had taken to calling me by Ray's old nickname shortly after Aurora had been born. I knew it was a way for her to keep Raylene's memory alive, and that Melody had lost the closest thing she had to a sister when my mate had died. It hadn't been hard for me to step into the role of Uncle and I knew that I would give my life to protect these two.

"Uncle Ric is doing as well as he can." I smiled down at the chubby face and chucked her lightly under the chin. It has been so long since I have been around a baby and I hadn't realized that I missed having a little one around. When the small girl squealed in delight I couldn't help smiling wider down at her, feeling the heaviness that plagued my heart lift just a little at the sound, the way it always did when I was around her.

"We are here for you, all you have to do is tell us what you need." Melody reached up and placed a hand on my arm.

I closed my eyes and leaned back against the door frame. What did I need? "I need her back." I whispered, "I need my mate, you need your best friend, your sister. What we both need, we can't have." I let the words fall from my mouth before I really thought them through, and I regretted them instantly. I closed my eyes and rubbed at them wearily.

"We all miss her, Ric." I could hear the sorrow in her voice and felt like I had been punched in the gut. I always end up feeling so guilty when we talk about Raylene, like I was being selfish grieving her for so long when I had known her for such a short time, especially compared to those who had come from her clan.

"I know." It was all I could say. I opened my eyes and laid my hands at the base of her spine to lead her from the office. If Melody was here I knew that it had to be getting close to dinner time, "How are things out there?" I asked as we made our way toward the dining room.

"It's going," she said with a sigh, "Everyone is trying to relearn to trust one another. There haven't been any more big fights though. A few squabbles here and there but others are starting to step in to calm things down. It's not always falling to Cali-Ann, Cal and the enforcers."

"I'm glad to hear that. The weekly outbreaks had me getting worried," I shook my head remembering when I had started to believe I would have to set harder boundaries about fighting. If it had been fights for dominance I would have been able to let it go, but since Marco's challenge six months ago there hadn't been a single fight for dominance in the pack. Instead, my people had begun to fight over the smallest slights. I had heard the excuses range from being bumped into while walking past each other to talking to someone else's girl-friend. After the first couple of months I had to step back from interfering as my presence seemed to make some of the fights worse, but I was glad that it had started to settle down.

"The fights seemed to have really started calming down once you reinstated the open dinners," she stopped just outside the dining room doors and turned to face me placing a hand on my arm, "they need to be able to see you Ric." Her voice was soft and the tone reminded me of her friend so much my heart clenched. "The dinners were a great start, it showed them that you were ok, but now they need to know that you are fully there for them still and not just when there is a problem. They need their King to be their King."

"I know Melody," I sighed and closed my eyes, pinching the bridge of my nose hoping to alleviate the growing headache. Raylene had warned me that being King would be different than being Alpha had been and she was right. Now Melody was right and I needed to fully step into the role I had agreed to. The thought of leading this barely united group still seems to be a near impossible task.

"Dinners ready your Majesty," Avianna's soft voice came from the doorway. She had taken up making dinner with Ryan whenever we have the open pack dinners which were normally three to four times a week. On the weeks that we had a fourth pack dinner, I had talked them into allowing me to order in one of the nights, but they still insisted on home cooked meals the rest of the time. I watched her eyes crease in worry as she took in the scene, "Is everything ok?"

My heart broke for the young Omega and I wished I could give her back the sister she lost, but I knew that if I ever saw Anabella again I would kill her for her part in Raylene's death. I walked over and pulled the small girl into a comforting hug, letting her lean into my side. For some reason Avianna's presence had always pulled out my Alpha side and made me feel like an overprotective big brother, "We are fine Avi. Melody was just catching me up on a few things. We will be inside in just a few minutes." I smiled down at her and gave her another soft squeeze, "And again, no need for the formalities."

"We can finish this after dinner," Mel smiled at Aviana and I loosened my hold on the Omega so she could proceed us into the half filled room. I had just stepped into the room when I heard the doorbell for the front door ring.

I sighed softly before looking at the others, "you guys go ahead and start. I will be back as soon as I see who that is and get rid of them."

Chapter 2

Sienna

I shouldered the duffle bag, gifted to me, filled with a weeks worth of donated clothing. I looked up at the tall man standing in front of me, "You are sure that I will be welcomed there?"

Alex shook his head, "I cannot guarantee you anything as I have not personally met the leader of the pack, but from everything I have heard of Alaric, he is the one most likely to welcome in a survivor without getting their full back story first. Rumor in our community is that his pack has many survivors that initially belonged to other packs or were turned and didn't have anywhere to go. Though as I have offered you are more than welcome to stay here with my pack Sienna."

I shook my head, "No, this is too close. He is already getting close to finding me while I've been here. I have to go. I have to get farther away from him if I want to be safe, if I want to keep my baby safe."

The shifter in front of me growled and I couldn't help but shrink away from him. He sighed and I could feel his frustration, "Have I not shown you that you are not in danger from me Sienna?" I had to fight my instincts to step away from him, to show him my fear. It wasn't really him I was afraid of, but the beast inside me told me to run, to protect myself from all Alpha's.

"I know that you won't hurt me, you helped me when I first escaped, but you are both a man and an Alpha Alex, I don't feel safe with any men, let alone the Alphas. I don't mean to upset you but you scare me, as do most of your pack, it's another reason that I have to go." my voice was barely above a whisper, but I couldn't bring myself to speak any louder over my fear.

"I understand," he closed his eyes and took a deep breath and I felt the air around him still, "I know that you have no reason to believe me, to believe any of us, but no sane Alpha would hurt an Omega." He set a hand on my shoulder and gave it a light squeeze before turning me toward the car that was waiting to take me to the train station and handed me a large envelope, "here is your train ticket, this will take you all the way to Seattle, and here is some cash to tide you over until you get on your feet there. When you get off the train I want you to get a private car to take you to the pack headquarters. Do not take any form of public transportation, do you understand me?" I nodded as he opened the door and helped me inside, "If you need anything you have my number along with my mate's, you can call either of us at any time."

I looked up at him from inside the back seat of the car, "I can't thank you enough for everything you have done." He gently squeezed the hand on my shoulder and I had to fight not to pull away. I knew that this was a compromise with him. Him and his Pack had shown me that touch between shifters was normal, but I still had not been able to accept it. A gentle shoulder squeeze was the compromise to the hugs and touches that came so naturally to the rest of them.

"You don't have to thank me for anything Sienna. You and that pup inside of you thriving is all I ask for." I nodded my thanks as I shoved the money into the duffle bag. When the door closed and I was alone in the back seat I let out the soft sigh. The driver of the car was one of the pack's human spouses, another compromise that they had made for me.

The train station was about a twenty minute drive from Alex's house and I spent the time forcing myself to go over what I would say to the new Alpha when I saw him.

Before I knew it we were pulling into the train station and the driver, I believe her name was Leslie, helped me leverage myself from the back seat. I wasn't used to the small but growing bulge of my stomach and already I could never seem to find my balance when transitioning from sitting to standing. I thanked her and made my way onto the train. After handing the ticket to the conductor at the train I quickly found the privacy cabin that Alex had gotten for me and settled myself inside of it, closing and locking the door immediately. I rubbed my hand over my belly as I looked out the window. Everything had changed so much in the last year. I never imagined I would ever leave California, but then again, I had never imagined I would become a monster either. I startled when the train lurched into motion but it didn't take long for the soft rumble of the train on the track to help lull me into one of the deepest sleeps I'd had in nearly a year.

***

The next day was longer than I expected as we made our way north. I kept the shades of my compartment closed except around meal times so that I wouldn't be startled by wait staff knocking to deliver my food. For most of the day I stayed in my small room, only slipping out to use the restroom at the end of the car. I napped off and on during the trip but as the sky grew dark I could feel my anxiety rising and sleep became a distant memory. It was as if the closer to the new pack I got the more restless my beast became. I waited for the sky outside to begin to lighten and changed into a clean set of clothes. I pulled the money out of the duffle bag and slid it into the front pocket of the jeans I had pulled on. I made sure I had everything packed into the duffle bag and was fully ready to depart by the time we reached the station. When we finally stopped in Seattle I waited until the flow of people had slowed before I slipped from the cabin and made my way out into the bright morning sunlight. After the crowd had dispersed I made my way over to one of the pay phones and called the number that Alex had given me to request a car to pick me up from the station. It took less than fifteen minutes for a shiny black car to pull up to the curb. I waited for the driver to confirm who they were to pick up and hold the door open for me before sliding into the back seat.

"Where are you off to Miss?" The chauffeur asked as his door clicked shut. I pulled the piece of paper from my pocket and read off the address that Alex had scribbled down for me. "Settle in, that's about an hour or so drive."

I tried to close my eyes and relax as we pulled away from the train station but my beast screamed at me from inside. Instead I spent the entire drive staring out the window, watching the city fade into rolling hills with subdivisions and then into a wooded more rural landscape.

When the car pulled into a long drive and stopped I looked down at the piece of paper in my hand and then back up at the house. Not a house, but a mansion. The place was huge. "You getting out Ma'am?" the driver asked and I nodded, passing him the last few dollars I had. The car had cost more than I expected and it had taken up everything that Alex had given me. Shouldering the duffle bag I slid from the car using the roof of the car to catch my balance before closing the door behind me. I took another look at the mansion, my hand falling to my stomach as I climbed up the steps to the large stone front porch. Sending a silent prayer to whoever was listening I pressed the small white button of the doorbell before clutching the strap of my bag and waiting.

The door opened to reveal a tall man with dark hair that looked like he had been running his hands through it and the most stunning green eyes I had ever seen. As he looked down at me my breath caught, and when he spoke I could feel a rush of excitement I hadn't felt in so long, "Can I help you?"

"I was looking for Alaric Preston, is he here?"

"I'm Alaric, I'm sorry, do I know you?" his brow furrowed as he continued to look down at me.

"Mr. Preston, Alex Docks told me that you would be able to help me." I spread my coat just enough for him to see the ever growing bump that was my stomach, "Please, I don't know where else to turn."

"Get inside out of the cold," his voice was nearly a growl this time and I couldn't help but shrink in on myself as I moved past him and into the large entry hall. I hated that this was how I reacted to anything even remotely aggressively male. I never used to cringe away from anything, but now I just wanted to curl into myself. "Why would Alex send you here? From what I have heard the Lake Tahoe pack takes in survivors just as we do. Where is your mate?"

"I don't have a mate, I needed to get out of California. I promise I am not a troublemaker, but I need help Mr. Preston. I was kidnapped a year ago and turned. When I found out I was pregnant I escaped to Alex's pack. With needing to leave California, Alex's pack was too close for me to feel safe. Now I just need somewhere to stay until I have my baby and then if you need me to leave I will. Please Mr. Preston." the words came out in a rush. I needed him to take me in. If he didn't I didn't know what else I could do.

"Alaric, my King, stop making that poor girl stand there shivering. Invite her to the dinner table and we can deal with the rest later" A small woman said from the doorway, a baby propped on her hip. She must be his mate.

The Alpha in front of me quirked an eyebrow at her and I couldn't stop myself from stepping back, stepping away from the potential violence, "Well, you heard Melody, it's time for dinner." Was the only response he gave before leading the way to a large and filled dining room. The woman with the infant sat next to an Alpha that was not Alaric as he had sat at the head of the table next to the only other empty seat. Slowly I made my way over and sat next to him.

I didn't reach for a plate, not sure if I could handle eating anything surrounded by so many people. After all of the bowls had been passed around the table once a full plate was set down in front of me. I looked up at the Alpha who had let me in and he lifted an eyebrow, giving the order to eat with just that simple motion. Not wanting to anger him and risk being put out on the street I picked up the biscuit he had put on there and pulled off a small section. I listened as the people, the shifters, around me talked about nothing and everything in their lives.The topics reminded me of that of a normal family. I still couldn't understand how such monsters could seem so normal, could hide in plain sight. I slid farther down in the seat, wanting to hide from every-one, from the dangers that were around me everywhere.

Chapter 3

Alaric

The small dark woman barely touched the food I had placed in front of her and seemed to draw further and further in around herself as dinner and conversations progressed. By the end of the meal my beast was growling at me to do something to make her feel more comfortable. I ignored it as best I could, waiting until I could see that every plate had been cleared or pushed away and then I stood, "If no one needs anything I will go get our guest settled and then retire for the night." I waited a moment or two to see if anyone had concerns they were brave enough to voice in front of our guest. I smiled reassuringly at everyone before gesturing to the door to the small woman.

I lifted her small duffle bag from the floor before she could attempt to heft it back onto her shoulder, frowning at how light it was, and led her through the house to the office. "I don't believe I caught your name," I said as I set the bag on one of the chairs across from the desk and closed the door behind us.

"Sienna" She said and her voice was just above a whisper. I watched as she huddled away from me and my beast raged, "Sienna Martinez."

"It is nice to meet you Sienna," I leaned against the desk and tucked my hands into my back pockets, trying to come off as non aggressive as possible. Which was hard when she was as tiny as she was and shivering like a scared rabbit. "I am willing to offer you shelter here, but I need to know that I am not putting my people in danger by doing so."

She shook her head, "I won't hurt anyone. I am just looking for somewhere to stay until

I can get on my feet and have my pup, somewhere that isn't California."

"When will the rest of your things arrive from California?" I asked, wondering if she would try to lie to me about the duffle bag being all she had or if she would come clean.

She looked down, her face going red and I almost felt bad asking, "I don't have anything else, just what's in the bag." I filed that away for later as something to talk to Melody about.

"And whatever you are running from? Will that come back to bite me in the ass?" She shrank away farther and wouldn't meet my eyes but shook her head. I didn't believe her, but I also couldn't bring myself to turn her away. I watched her wrap her arms protectively around her stomach as if to protect her baby and I fought back a growl. She was terrified of something and I didn't want to add to that fear. "Sienna, I can offer you shelter but I cannot offer you a place in the pack." I held up a hand to soothe the look of panic that filled her eyes, "I run my pack as a democracy. I will allow you to stay until your pup reaches six months, after that time it will go to the pack to vote if you become a member or if you will need to move on. If that happens we will help you relocate to a pack of your choice that will take you in, or if you decide that you wish to be a lone wolf we can also help you get set up somewhere away from other groups. That being said, if you cause any problems for my pack you will be told to leave immediately," I waited for her to nod her understanding, "Now, I think it's time for bed. If you can follow me I will show you to a room."

I led her through the house and to one of the guestrooms just down the hall from my own room so that I could keep an ear out for her. I opened the door and stepped back to let her in. I had to clench my fists to keep myself from reaching out to her as she passed by me, the waves of terror radiating from her nearly making her tremble. I wanted to pull her into my arms, to soothe her as I would for any of my shifters, but something told me that touching her would only further her fear. She wasn't like most of the shifters I knew who seemed to crave touch and comfort, instead she seemed to want to avoid it at all costs, "If you need anything just ask anyone here and they will be more than willing to help you." I stepped out of the room, closing the door behind me as I did.

"Alaric," Melody's voice was soft, "Can we talk?" I turned to find her down the hallway a little near the stairs.

"Of course," I moved to her, frowning in concern, "Do you want to go to the living room or the office?"

"I think maybe we should walk," she smiled. I let her move first, following as she led me back down the stairs before beginning to wander almost aimlessly through the large house. For several minutes we moved in silence, "I miss her, but I didn't cut myself off from making new friends." I frowned at her words, more confused than ever by the start of this conversation, "I know Raylene wouldn't have wanted me to do that." Her voice was soft. "Cal saw it too, by the way, so I'm not just trying to play matchmaker here. Your beast called for you to protect that girl at dinner. Your beasts call to one another, and you shouldn't go through life alone."

Suddenly the words she was saying clicked in my brain and my chest clenched at the suggestion, "I'm not ready Melody." I sighed and ran a hand through my hair, "Truth be told I don't know if I will ever be ready. I have lost everyone I have ever loved, and I don't know if I could handle going through that again. Losing Raylene brought back all of the pain of losing Kate and the kids. I don't want to go through that again, ever." We stopped outside the room to the suite that Melody and her small family now lived in. "I have loved twice in my life, and I have lost both loves in a way that I wouldn't wish on anyone. After losing Kate I never expected to find someone who I could give my heart to again, but then Raylene stormed in and something in me healed.

When I held her in my arms that part of me that she healed died with her. I can't expect the universe to give me a third chance. I don't deserve it."

When she stepped forward and wrapped her arms around me I hesitated for a moment before hugging her tightly, "Just don't let fear of possible loss stop you from the possibility of happiness," She said softly before letting go and stepping back. "Also, I'm not saying that you need to find another epic love, but I do want you to find happiness." She smiled up at me one last time before heading into her room. I stood outside the door for a minute, resting my forehead against the frame, but I couldn't calm my beast. I needed to run. I made my way back through the house until I was on the back porch and stepped from my clothes. I took two running steps and launched myself from the top of the stairs, letting the magic of the change wrap itself around me before landing on four paws.

I looked up and could see the light on in the room I had settled Sienna into. I stood still for a moment and strained my ears until I heard the water running in the house from that direction. Assured that she was inside and safe I set off at a lope around the large house, slowly circling out farther and farther before darting off into the woods. There are times that shifting clears the mind in a way that humans just could never understand, a way I had never understood until I finally let myself become one with my beast. After meeting this woman and Melody's conversation, a run was the only way to clear my mind. When my paws hit the dirt under the canopy of trees I gave myself over to the beast and the feeling of the night around me.

I ran until the moon was high overhead and my paws ached from the minute scratches the wood's undergrowth gave. I ran until my muscles ached and I panted tongue lolling out. I only returned to the house when the only thoughts in my head were crawling into my bed. Shifting back once I was halfway across the yard I stumbled my way to the back porch and to my room. Once there I fell face down on the bed and let the exhaustion sweep me away.

Chapter 4

Sienna

I looked around the room after the door closed and I turned the lock on the handle. The walls were a light grayish blue, almost the color of fresh snow. The floor was the same dark wood that I had found through the rest of the house, and under the bed was a thick rug that looked like my feet would sink into when I walked on it. On either side of the bed were small nightstands, each of which held a small lamp with a white shade. Then there was the bed itself. It was a black canopy frame, though the sides had been left empty. The head and footboard looked to be padded and covered in what looked to be leather. The bed was made with a light gray comforter with a folded fur like blanket at the end. The headboard was piled with pillows. All of it made me want to crawl into the bed and never leave it. There was a large window with two gray leather barrel arm chairs that sat to either side of it, a small round table sat between them. In the corner of the room not too far from the door was a small writing desk with a straight back chair pushed in underneath.

Even before Kevin, I had never been in a room this big. My first apartment had been the size of this one room. I opened the duffle bag and pulled out the nightgown and gold knife that Alex had given me. I grabbed the chair from by the desk and brought it into the bathroom with me. The bathroom was larger than any bathroom I'd ever seen outside of the movies. The shower was a walk-in shower that took up the corner farthest from the door with glass blocks separating it from the rest of the room. Next to the shower, closer to the door was an old style black clawfoot tub that was definitely large enough for me to fully soak into even with my five month pregnant stomach. Across from both of them was a long black counter with silver veining running through it. The entire wall above the counter was one large mirror, and above the counter was a crystal like chandelier. Closing the door, I wedged the chair under the handle before I started to undress. I laid the nightgown on the long counter along with my clothes as I pulled them off. Stepping to the shower I laid the glinting blade on the back of the toilet that was tucked next to the shower at the end of the counter before turning on the water and stepping under the spray.

I nearly groaned in ecstasy as the water heated, the pounding spray relaxing the muscles that had been tense for so long. I stood under the spray long after I had finished washing myself, long after my skin had begun to pucker from the water. I didn't turn the water off until my knees were nearly buckling from exhaustion, wanting to soak up as much of the heat as I could. When I could barely keep my eyes open I turned the water off and reached over for the large white fluffy towel that was on the heated towel rack. I ruffled my hair dry, still not used to how short it was. I missed my long hair and still mourned it every time I ran a brush through the dark strands. Once it was no longer dripping I pulled on the nightgown and picked up the knife and my dirty clothes. I pressed my ear to the door, listening for anyone who may have entered the bedroom while I was in the shower. After a few minutes of hearing nothing there I pulled the chair away from the door and slowly opened it. When I had again confirmed it was empty I turned the light off in the bathroom. I set everything from my arms onto the bed and went back to the bathroom for the chair. I then moved the chair over to the bedroom's main door and propped it under the handle.

I turned on the small white lamp next to the bed and checked that the huge walk-in closet was empty before setting my duffle bag just inside of the door on the floor. I grabbed the small journal from under the clothes, closing the door. Slipping the knife between the mattress and box spring I crawled under the thick gray comforter. I leaned my back against the padded headboard and added notes to the journal with what the day had held for me. I wrote down everything that scared me and why, just as the shifter therapist from Alex's pack had suggested. I thought over each situation and contemplated how I would have handled them in my old life, and how I wished I could handle them now. After a few minutes I set the journal on the nightstand and turned, shifting the pillows until I could curl up with my back to the headboard. Finally, I let my eyes close and drifted to sleep, with my knees pulled up around my stomach as best I could to protect the life I was growing.

***

I startled awake from memories of cold steel bars digging into my skin, to a soft knock on the door and threw myself off the opposite side of the bed, huddling behind it. I darted my eyes to the walk-in closet and wondered if I would be safer in there.

"Sienna?" I heard the Alpha's voice call softly through the door, his voice was filled with what sounded like concern.

"Y-yes sir?" I called back trying to force myself to calm down.

"Is everything ok?"

"Everything is fine, I w-was just startled by the knock waking me up."

"I apologize. I didn't mean to scare you. I just wanted to let you know that breakfast was ready whenever you would like to join us." Breakfast. That meant other people. It meant leaving the safety of this room, of my solitude.

"Sienna, you don't have to come down, I just wanted you to know that food was available. You and your baby need the nutrition, but I can have a tray brought up and set outside the door for you." I was becoming a nuisance. I had to pull myself together, I couldn't make him angry. I needed a safe place to stay. My baby needed a safe place to stay. I was suffocating. Why couldn't I get enough air? There was something around my chest squeezing, not allowing me to take a full breath. I whimpered as panic gripped me. I could hear the Alpha's voice still muffled by the door. I pressed into the wall as far from the voice as I could get, gasping for air, needing to breathe. I could feel my fingers clawing at my throat but it was as if I had no control over them. When I heard the door crash open something inside of me cracked and I curled around my stomach having to protect the baby inside of me. "Sienna," His voice was so much closer, but he didn't sound angry. That wasn't right though, of course the Alpha was angry I hadn't come when he had told me to. I didn't come and he would beat me for my disobedience, "Sienna, you have to breathe or you are going to pass out." I looked up at him through a blur of tears, his green eyes filled with what seemed to be concern as he peered at me from inches away. That wasn't right, his eyes were brown not green. "Slow your breathing Sienna, you have to calm yourself." His voice was slow and calm, even though his eyes were wild, "Match your breaths with mine, come on now," I watched as he took in a slow deep breath, chest expanding. I felt my own chest expanding, matching his and filling with air that I desperately needed. After a few minutes I shuddered and slumped back against the wall exhausted. "Hey are you ok?" He whispered to me. I looked up at him through the hair that had fallen across my face.

"I'm sorry," my voice was a barely audible rasp.

"You have nothing to be sorry about. You had a panic attack, it happens. As long as you are ok and we can figure out what the trigger was, we can work through it." A panic attack, I closed my eyes and fought back a sob of anger and frustration. I'd had yet another panic attack. I hated that I was this weak. "You want to come down for food? It will just be me and you and three others who live here."

"May I get dressed first?" I whispered.

"Of course, use the bathroom and pack up your bag, I will move you to another room, the door will need to be fixed on this one." I opened my eyes and peeked up over the bed to see that the door had been forced open, the wall around it was cracked and splintered. I looked up at him, eyes wide. He shrugged and his pale cheeks seemed to almost tint in embarrassment, "I could feel your fear, I thought something had happened." he shrugged again as if it hadn't been a big deal. I nodded and slowly stood. "I'll be waiting for you downstairs. We are going to eat in the back sunroom, so I can show you the way."

"I won't be long, I'm sorry for causing such distress here already," I mumbled as I grabbed my bag from the closet.

"It's fine. Once you have been here for a bit, it will get better." I nodded and watched him leave the room before locking myself in the bathroom, a fresh wave of tears slipping down my face. This time in sheer embarrassment and shame.

Chapter 5

Alaric

"Hey Ric?" Melody said from the doorway to the office.

"Hmm?" I didn't look up, still trying to understand the numbers on the screen that Raylene had manipulated so easily. She had always been a wonder when it came to pack finances, and pack politics, and knowing when to hold their hands or when to push them. She had been so perfect at handling everything. Raylene had been such a natural leader that I still didn't know how I could possibly live up to her legacy.

"It's mid-moon, we were thinking it was a good time to get the pack together for a cookout, especially with winter coming up."

I looked up at her, "Are you actually asking my permission for a cookout?"

She laughed, "You are so funny. No, I was letting you know that I just sent Cal to the butcher for burgers and brats and that Cali-Ann called saying she was bringing the Bedal group down."

I shook my head and laughed, "You two are a pain in my ass you know that right?"

"You wouldn't have us any other way." she grinned back, "I figured that this might also be a time to introduce Sienna to more of the pack." She said, her voice growing more serious, "She's been here for nearly a week now and If she wants to stay, people have to actually know she exists."

I saved what I was doing and stood with a nod, "I'll go talk to her, do you know where she is?" I asked, stretching my arms out over my head, wondering if there was a chiropractor for shifters, or maybe I needed to suck it up and get back to working on cars and not a computer.

"In the library, I think it has become her favorite room besides her own."

I laughed softly and nodded, "I should have figured, I will go talk to her and give her a heads up." I stood with a slight shake to my head knowing that the information I am about to impart on Sienna will cause fear and anxiety, hating that her reaction will automatically be fear and anxiety. Our pack for the most part is just a really large blended family. I just needed to figure out how to help Sienna incorporate herself into the family.

***

I leaned against the doorframe of the library and watched as Sienna slowly moved along one of the dark wood, floor to ceiling full wall shelves, her finger tracing over the titles on the spines of the leather bound books. She paused and I saw her smile as she pulled the book free. It was a small smile, barely visible, but it held a hint of what it would have been like before whatever tragedy had touched her, changed her. It was the first hint of happiness I had seen her display since she had shown up on my doorstep nearly a week ago. She pulled out the book a few titles down from the last and tucked it into the crook of her arm, along with the two books next to it. I knocked softly on the door frame and my heart clenched when she jumped. It seems like no matter how I approach a room she's in, I startled her.

"I didn't mean to frighten you." I kept my voice soft and neutral, the tone I would use with a frightened animal.

She shrugged a little, her shoulders hunching as I watched, "It's ok, I just was engrossed in the books. Did you need me to do something?" She asked, clutching the books to her chest.

"I've told you before Sienna, there is nothing here that you are required to do other than to take care of yourself and the pup inside of you. I was just coming by to let you know that a large portion of the pack will be coming over in a little while." I watched her begin to build the wall that she seemed to keep around herself higher and I wanted to sigh, "I know that you aren't comfortable with large groups of peo- ple, but if you want to stay with this pack you have to get to know them and let them get to know you. You don't have to join the group on the lawn, but if you at least come out to the porch it would allow them to see you, and eventually get to know you." I watched her chew her lip in thought.

"I can stay on the porch?" I could see her worrying the spine on one of the books in her hands.

I nodded, "You can even bring a book out with you if you would like. I know that groups make you anxious, I have noticed that every time someone enters a room you startle. There is nothing wrong with that, but I think if you were to be around us a little more, it may make things more comfortable for you." I didn't mention the fact that it would allow her animal side to also acclimate to ours, which was important with the upcoming full moon. Acclimating her animal side to our pack will create an instinctual bond to prevent any altercations in animal form, even if it wouldn't help her in human form.

She chewed her lip more as she thought over my words. After a few moments she nodded and I saw her eyes fill with a resolve I hadn't seen in her yet, "Ok, I'll try to come out with everyone."

I smiled encouragingly at her, "Remember, you can always come back inside any time you start to feel uncomfortable." She nodded. "I'm gonna go help get things set up, and I'll see you outside." I stepped back from the door and left her to continue her book browsing.

***

As the backyard filled I could feel my more animalistic urges settle and calm. Most of the pack had shown up and the smell of fresh meat on the grill filled the air. I leaned back in a chair down on the lawn, it was nearly a perfect day, the only thing that ruined it was the aching empty hole in my chest where Raylene used to be. Unconsciously I looked to the porch and must have frowned not seeing Sienna out yet.

"Well don't you look all grumpy" Cali-Ann said, stepping up next to me and propping her hip on the arm of my chair.

"And you are still a pain in my ass." I looked up at her with a lifted eyebrow, "How is Be-dal?"

"You're missed, but many understand why you are choosing to spend more time here."

I nodded, "Winter is coming and I'll be back there more often again, the shop will be getting busy."

"Workaholic" she grinned and ruffled my hair before heading out to mingle. I rolled my eyes at her antics but couldn't help but smile. She reminded me too much of the sister I had left behind.

***

For a moment I wasn't on the patio in Washington but on a different patio in the desert of New Mexico. I was watching Kate chase Ty around, fingers wiggling in a tickling motion as the toddler ran away screeching in laughter. Katerina sat on the arm of my chair, one of mom's wine coolers in her hand.

"I don't think I have ever seen you look so relaxed and happy big brother," she teased, reaching out to ruffle my hair.

"And I don't think you are old enough to be drinking this." I said reaching over to take the frosted bottle from her hand.

"Spoilsport," she pouted and got up to wander back inside, probably hoping to sneak another bottle from the fridge without being caught.

***

"Hey Alpha, wanna play ball?" one of the shifters asked, tossing a football up and down pulling me back to the present.

I glanced over to the porch and saw that Sienna had come out and was wrapped in a large black sweater, curled up in one of the wicker couches. She held a book in her lap, but instead of reading it she seemed to be using it as more of a comfort object. I checked that none of my more overzealous shifters were in the vicinity before standing up, "Yeah sure why not," I grinned my answer to them and pulled my T-shirt over my head, dropping it to the chair. I rolled my neck to loosen my shoulders, letting the excitement of a little backyard rivalry fill me. It isn't often enough that I get to mingle with the pack purely for entertainment.

The biggest difference playing backyard ball with shifters than when I was human was that touch football wasn't even an option. We always played full contact. It wasn't too long until I had caught the ball thrown directly to me and I was suddenly on the bottom of a dog pile. I finally pulled myself free from the others, laughing hard enough that it nearly hindered my struggle to freedom. When I regained my feet I felt a wave of fear from the direction of the porch. Quickly my laughter cut off and I grabbed my shirt pulling it on as

I jogged to where I saw Aviana sitting next to a weary looking Sienna.

Chapter 6

Sienna

I was sitting on an outdoor wicker couch on the large back enclosed porch, an over-sized black sweater pulled around my shoulders against the chilly fall air. I watched a large group of shifters, mostly Alphas, begin playing what looked to be a very energetic game of shirts vs skins football in the large back yard. A part of me let out what felt like a purr when I saw Alaric pull his shirt over his head and drop it to the ground in one smooth motion. Even after everything I could admit, at least to myself, that the man was the definition of eye candy. He was the type of guy my sister and I would have giggled over at the mall a little over a year ago. I smiled wistfully at the memory and ached for that feeling of family that had always been there.

"Hi," a cheery voice said from next to me. I startled pulling myself in tighter before turning to find a small young woman smiling brightly at me from the end of the couch. Her heart shaped face was framed by beautiful, wavy flowing brown hair that she left to hang loose and pulled attention to her large strikingly bright blue eyes. I recognized her as someone who was regularly at the dinners that Alaric encouraged me to join in on. Alaric seemed to always show her signs of affection and part of me searched to find any similarities between them that would signify their relationship. "I'm Avianna, I tend to help out a lot with the cooking since my mate and I run a small bakery about two hours from here. Melody mentioned that you were hoping to join the pack, I think that would be great." She looked over her shoulder smiling as several of the Alpha let out whooping victory cries, "They can be a bit much, huh?" she said sitting down at the opposite end of the couch from me.

"They are definitely intimidating" I mumbled tucking myself even tighter into the corner of the couch. I was missing the safety I had begun to feel in my room upstairs and even in the luxurious library but Alaric had pointed out that the pack couldn't grant me permission to join if they didn't know I existed. Forcing myself to take slow deep breaths I tried to calm myself. I knew I shouldn't feel worried or anxious around her, but the last year has not given me much opportunity to make friends or even feel comfortable in the presence of others. I still feel like I am surrounded by monsters, monsters like I am now.

Avianna tilted her head a little as she looked at me, "Do you want to get out of here? We could get away from all the guys and just have some girl time. Maybe we could go shopping.

I heard you were expecting, we could go get a few things for you and the baby."

I felt my cheeks burn red, "I don't have any money, I'm still looking for a job." I couldn't bring myself to speak louder than a whisper and part of me wished that the chirpy girl next to me would just go away. I knew that she was just trying to be polite but admitting out loud that I was dependent on these strangers for everything made me want to run and hide even more.

"The pack has plenty of money to get you and the baby basic's. Alaric is an amazing Alpha, and Raylene was an amazing leader before him. In this pack, we take care of each other. We are kinda like a big family and family helps family." She made the comments as if it meant nothing that a stranger would come in and expect to be taken care of. All of the talk of family did not apply to me, I wasn't part of the pack, I was a stranger.

"You don't know me, I'm a complete stranger. Why would you want to help me?" I knew the words that left my mouth were rude but I didn't get it. I was a stranger and had brought nothing to this group of people who all acted as if they were one large family.

"Because you are a shifter in need. You came to us for help Sienna, and safety, let us help you. You are only a stranger for now. If you let us, we would like to at least be your friends." Avianna looked at me, eyes full of emotions that I couldn't comprehend. "We want to get to know you, give us a chance. Most of the shifters in this pack are pretty awesome people."

"I'm scared. This last year has changed everything, my entire life was ripped away from me and I don't know how to handle any of it." I shivered and wished I had something warmer than the black sweater, "I used to trust people, I used to like going out shopping and doing things. Now, I'm scared. I am scared of everything and everyone, especially men and Alphas."

"Then no Alphas today," she smiled, "I will talk to Ryan and Alaric."

"I thought Omega's weren't allowed to go out without an Alpha." I said. I couldn't seem to get my head to wrap around all the rules of being a shifter. They never seemed to stay the same, as if they were made to trip you up and cause you to receive punishment.

"It's not that we aren't allowed to, we aren't prisoners Sienna, most of us just enjoy the company of our Alpha. We enjoy being around them the way a normal human enjoys being around the person they love."

"I don't understand any of this," I could feel my throat closing as my eyes started to fog with tears. My life didn't make sense anymore. This world I have been forced into made no sense, "I have heard and seen and been told so many different and conflicting rules. I don't know how to do this, be this. To be a shifter, a mon-ster" The last word was just above a breath but I could see Avianna jerk back as if she had been hit. Within moments Alaric and another

Alpha were there in front of us. Instinctively I pulled my knees as close to my chest as I could without putting pressure on my stomach.

"Is everything ok over here?" the second Alpha asked as he moved to rub his hand comfortingly along Avianna's shoulders. I could see a crowd forming behind the three shifters in front of me and I wanted to run but I had allowed myself to be cornered.

"We aren't monsters," Avianna said softly leaning against the man, "you aren't a monster. I don't know what you went through before you got here. What I do know though is that you will never learn to be the shifter you can be if you think of yourself as a monster." She stood and let herself be pulled into the man's arms, "let me know if you decide you want to go on that shopping trip." She sent a weak smile over to me before letting the man lead her away with a comforting arm around her shoulders holding her close.

"Alright, everyone disperse. There's nothing to see here," A small bombshell blonde said as she started to wave everyone away.

"Are you ok?" Alaric's voice was soft as he dropped to his knees in front of me. Having others feel what I am feeling still seems so strange, I feel like I wear fear and anxiety like a coat that everyone can see.

"I don't know." The words caught in my throat and came out with a sob, "I don't know what is happening. I don't know how to be anything but scared of everything." I tucked my face against my legs as I cried, "I never used to be scared and now I'm always scared. You scare me, the guy who made Avianna feel safe scares me. I scare me." I felt something drape over my shoulders and the couch dip next to me.

"You obviously went through something horrific," Alaric's voice was gentle, "I understand what that's like. I don't know what you went through, but I know that you have a right to feel all of your feelings. You also have a right to find someplace to be safe." I could feel my pulse slowing as he talked, could feel myself calming in a way I hadn't since before my attack, "Why don't you go up to your room, take some time to feel safe again. I'll get everyone rounded up and sent on their way and we can have a quiet dinner tonight ok?" I looked up at him from over my arms and nodded slowly. "Anything in particular that you want?"

"Gyro?" I whispered softly. When he laughed the sound wrapped around me and I felt warmer than I had even with the added blanket.

"Go inside and I will see what I can do." He smiled softly before standing and making his way back out to the backyard with a sharp whistle.

Chapter 7

Alaric

I passed the word to Cali-Ann to get every-one moving out and for the remainder of the burgers and brats to be put in the walk-in freezer for the full moon before going in search of dinner for the night for Sienna and myself. After a few phone calls I found that the pack's favorite pizza place also did gyros and ordered them for the two of us. I was just ushering the last couple of pack members to the door when the delivery driver pulled up.

"Not as much food as you normally order Mr. Preston sir," the young kid grinned as he handed me the takeout bag.

I smiled as I passed him a more than generous tip, "I decided on not having the entire family over tonight."

"Well you have a good night sir," I waited until the gate closed behind him before heading back into the house.

I stopped at the bottom of the stairs and called up them softly, "Sienna food's here if you wanna come down, I'll be in the kitchen." I didn't wait for a response but instead headed toward the kitchen in the back of the house. I pulled a couple of paper plates from the cabinet and silverware from the drawer. When I turned Sienna was standing in the doorway and was still wearing the oversized black sweater. The garment was so large on her that one side of the neck was hanging off her shoulder. She had one arm crossed over her stomach holding her other arm as she chewed her lip while looking up at me from under lowered lashes. I sent a comforting smile her way as I continued to set everything on the small table that was in the kitchen. I let her continue to stand watching me as I set the table, even going as far as to pull out a couple larger plates to pile the Gyro and sides onto. Once there was nothing left for me to do I walked over to her, stopping about a foot in front of her. My wolf growled when she hunched in on herself, pulling back from me. I ignored my wolf side and took a single step back, a step away from her, "Sienna" I said her name softly and waited for her to lift her gaze to mine again, "I can calm you if you want. It's part of what I can do as an Alpha, and as pack leader, but I won't unless you want me to."

She chewed her lip a little more, "I'm afraid." She sounded like a little girl, voice soft and timid.

"I don't want you to be afraid, especially not of me, but I won't take your emotions from you. Why don't we start by just sitting down and having dinner? You have to start eating more, not only because as a shifter you need more food, but to keep that baby inside healthy." She nodded and moved past me to sit at the table. I stayed still until I heard her chair slide close to the table and then I turned and walked to the table, sitting across from her. She had a half-filled pita on her plate and maybe half a dozen french fries. I shook my head and grabbed the serving tongs to fill her plate. I added more meat to the pita until the small wafer of bread couldn't hold anymore and piled on the fries until they were nearly falling off her plate. "You need to finish every-thing there." I said keeping my voice soft while still making sure she knew I was serious. Again she nodded before picking up her fork and starting her ritualistic picking and nibbling. I filled my own plate, deciding to leave the fries for her and instead opted for the onion rings. I waited till she had eaten about half of what I had given her before trying again to start a conversation.

"Why did you come here Sienna? Of all the packs in the United States, in the world even, why did you come here?" She took a deep breath and set her fork down. Instantly I regretted not waiting until she had fully finished the food that I had given her.

"This was the closest pack to where I escaped from other than Alex's in Lake Tahoe. I needed to go north from there, I figured it would be the least likely route for me to take, at least in his mind."

"Who is he?" I kept my voice gentle even as the beast inside me screamed to kill whoever it was to keep her safe.

She sighed and closed her eyes, "I guess I should tell you what happened if I expect you to let me stay here amongst your pack." She looked up at me and I could see the pain in her eyes, "I can't eat anymore, please. Especially not if you want me to tell you this story."

I nodded and stood collecting the dishes, "I'll clean up here. Why don't you choose a room and we can sit and you can tell me what happened." She nodded and slid back from the table before scurrying out of the room. I gave her a few minutes while I cleaned up dinner before letting my nose follow her scent.

I fought not to rush to her, I forgot how much seeking out a shifter like this triggered the same feeling as hunting a wounded deer in the woods. I found her in the library curled up in the corner of a leather couch. I couldn't stop my breath from catching as I watched the flickering light of the fire in the fireplace dance over her dark eyes and hair. I softly cleared my throat trying not to startle her, but she still jumped and tightened in around herself.

I moved in and sat on the couch at the opposite end from her, "I won't push Sienna, but I will listen to anything you want to tell me."

She nodded and looked back into the fire. I waited silently and after a few moments she began to speak, her soft voice filling the room, "I had stayed late at work, trying to make sure everything was ready for the Thanksgiving break. When you work in a hospital's billing department things can get backed up over a four-day weekend. Anyway, I was the last one in the office and had just finished closing down the building and locking everything up. My car was parked under a light like usual, just the way I had been taught if it was going to be dark when I would leave at night," she laughed softly, but I could hear the mocking tone that it held. "I even had my keys between my fingers. I felt fire cut across my back, I think I screamed, but honestly, I'm not sure. Next thing I know I'm waking up locked in a damn metal dog cage in the corner of a bedroom." her voice filled with a fire I had yet to hear from her and it gave me hope. "I was still wearing my scrubs, they were shredded and covered in blood, my blood as it turned out." I could feel her panic rising over that flicker of anger and wanted to reach out to comfort her, "I don't know how long I was there. I yelled and screamed for help but no one came. When he first walked into the room I thought he had heard me from outside and was coming to let me out, to save me. He let me out, and as soon as I opened my mouth to thank him he hit me. He hit me so hard I fell and my face slammed into the wall. He said he was tired of my screaming, that women were to be seen and not heard. That he wouldn't have some loud mouth bitch in his house." She bit back a soft sob. "That first day he used a belt on me. He hit me with it over and over as I begged for mercy. He never stopped, not even when my skin split open. He didn't stop until I stopped screaming because I couldn't anymore. When I was nothing but a whimpering ball, he yanked me up by my hair and threw me on the bed. He told me that the only time I was to scream was when he was using me the way a whore was meant to be used. And then he raped me." Her voice broke and my beast howled inside of me, "I couldn't fight him. When he had finished he pushed me to the floor and kicked me until I crawled back into the cage. I don't know if I blacked out or fell asleep, but when I woke up my wounds from the beating had healed." She looked over to me and I could see the terror in her eyes and again had to keep myself from pulling her into me.

"It was the same thing every night. Eventually he stopped locking me in the cage, but instead would lock me to the foot of the bed like a dog. When my first full moon came and I changed he was ecstatic. I had never been so scared and confused as I was that first full moon. After he turned he tore into me with teeth and claws." She had begun to tremble and I could no longer keep myself back from her and slid closer letting just a touch of my calming magic seep out and around her. "He did that every full moon, until the last two. Once he learned I was pregnant he stopped the beatings, and he stopped hurting me on the full moons. The second one I waited until he had dug into the dead animal he had brought home and I ran. I jumped through the window and I ran. I somehow ended up running into Alex's pack and the next morning when we were all waking back up, I woke up to Alex and his enforcers standing over me. I was terrified, he always told me that any shifters near us would bring me back to him, that they have all been made aware that I was his property. We went to their pack house, he got me clothes and food. I was so hungry; Kevin, that was his name, would only bring me scraps every other day or so. I told Alex what happened, he offered me asylum in his pack. I tried. I was there for about a week but I was so scared he would find me again. I knew if I went south, back towards home he would find me. So I asked Alex where I should go, and here I am." She looked up at me and my heart broke.

"I want to comfort you Sienna. Shifters, we are a touchy bunch, so my inclination right now as both a shifter and as an Alpha seeing an Omega in distress is to reach out for you and try to comfort you. I won't though unless you are ok with it." I waited until she slowly nodded her head and closed the distance between us. I lifted my arm and let her curl herself against my side. I let my arm slowly drape over her, feeling her stiffen before slowly relaxing again. I felt her body tremble as she sobbed into my side and I sat quietly letting her. I would make sure that my people knew she was now one of ours to protect. There would be no vote, I would make this ruling as King.

Chapter 8

Sienna

When Alaric raised his arm and let me settle against him I could feel a calm wash over me, but there was still a small voice in the back of my head screaming at me to run. It urged me to get as far away from the scent of Alpha as I could, but another voice said that we didn't need to run. That one was strong and calm, it told me that this calm and safe feeling is what it was supposed to be like when around an Alpha. I couldn't stop the panic when his arm settled over me, trapping me against him and had to take slow breaths to force myself to relax again. As I relaxed into his side I felt his hand start to make long, slow, soothing strokes up and down my back. Slowly I let my eyes drift close and sunk into the feeling of being held by someone safe.

"Don't worry about the pack," his voice was soft and calm when he finally spoke, "I will make it clear to them that you are to stay here, under our protection, until you decide you no longer wish to stay." I stiffened again, I didn't want everyone knowing my tragic history, "I won't tell them any details, I won't have to."

I looked up at him as another dreaded idea settled into my stomach, "I won't take a mate. I can't be forced to tie myself to someone." Flashes of teeth scraping against my throat and whispered threats filled me with renewed dread. Immediately I wondered if I should just run again and hide alone with me and my baby.

"Hey easy there, No one is going to force you to do anything. No one in this pack is with a mate that they did not willingly choose and that is the way things will continue to run."

He met my gaze, eyes calm and steady, "This pack is like a family Sienna, and I won't let anyone hurt my family." He gave a soft tug and I settled back into his side. Slowly he started to rub my back in a slow soothing gesture, "Avianna is right about several things though. We aren't monsters, you are not a monster, the person who kidnapped you was the monster. You also need to get more things for both you and the baby. There is no way that there is enough in that tiny duffle bag you came here with to last you for any length of time."

"I don't want to go out. I'm starting to feel safe here, and I don't want to go out where I won't feel safe. And I don't want an escort of Alphas that make me feel even more scared than I already am, and I don't have money." Again my cheeks flamed in embarrassment.

"Then don't go out shopping, you can shop online, from the comfort of your room. You can use my computer, and as for money you can use the packs card for the purchases. We have a bank account just for times like this when a pack member is in need, and you are now a pack member Sienna."

"I don't want anyone thinking I am trying to take advantage of your hospitality."

"Then we will work something out for you to pay back the pack either when you feel comfortable getting a job or by working for the pack in some way. Did you like the financial aspect of your job? What did you like about what you did at the hospital? I know you said you worked in the hospital but what did you do in your free time?"

I thought back to my life before the abduction, it had been so long since I had let myself think of it. "I come from a big family." Just mentioning them I felt a smile tug at my lips, "My mom has two sisters and three brothers, my dad has four sisters. I have two younger sisters and an older brother. We have close to twenty cousins between the two sides. When I," I hesitated, I hated the word kidnapped, it always reminded me of how weak I was "left, my brother had two kids, a boy and a girl." I smiled thinking of my niece and nephew, "And my youngest sister had just gotten married and was pregnant with her first child. I don't know if it was a boy or girl."

"Well now you've told me about your family, what about you?" Alaric prodded gently.

I laughed a little, "There isn't much to tell about me. In high school I kept my head down and focused on my school work. As soon as I graduated I started college right away, taking classes in the summer semester. I went to school for medical coding. I chose it not because it's what I always dreamed of doing but because it was a guaranteed job. I got into the local hospital about a year after high school graduation. I got my own apartment within six months and even chose one just down the block from the hospital so I could walk. After that I just kinda fell into a routine, work home, work home, and stopping at the grocery store every friday." I felt tears slip down my cheeks, "I hadn't even realized how much of my life I had wasted until it was gone." The last words were a sob. Alaric hugged me close to him, his hand rubbing soothingly up and down my arm as I wept for the life I had never gotten to live. I wasn't sure how long I stayed there in his arms, finally mourning the loss of my life. I didn't even realize when the tears stopped and I stayed there just for comfort until eventually I drifted off into an exhausted sleep.

***

I blinked sleepily as I felt myself being lifted into a pair of muscled arms. "Go back to sleep, I'm just going to lay you in bed," Alaric's voice soothed quietly. Yawning I tucked my face in against his chest and let myself drift in and out as he carried me down the halls. I buried my nose against him and a small part of me thought how much better it would have been if he hadn't been wearing the thin t-shirt, how much better it would have been to rub our cheek against his bare chest. When we got to the room I pushed myself from his arms, my pulse suddenly racing as soon as he stepped over the threshold. It was as if being in the same room as an Alpha and a bed had my anxiety soaring back up.

"Thank you," I whispered softly, stepping back from him as soon as my feet touched the floor. I wrapped my arms around myself and suddenly the smell of him that was moments ago soothing had my stomach roiling.

"You're welcome, hopefully one day you will trust me Sienna. I won't hurt you and I won't let anyone else here hurt you either." He stepped out of the room and closed the door behind him. Trembling slightly I crawled into the big bed, once again shifting to press my back against the headboard and turning on the small table lamp. I cocooned myself in the blankets, rubbing my cheek along the soft fur of what was quickly becoming my favorite blanket before drifting back into a deep sleep. With the Alphas scent still lingering in my nose I felt as if I was being held in a warm safety net.

Chapter 9

Alaric

I leaned back in the chair listening to the buzz of the pack around me. After we lost Raylene I had decided to continue the get together between full moons. As it had when we first brought our packs together, it seemed to have helped to heal the divide her death and those who caused it had left. Like with any large family we still have our squabbles, and damned if I wasn't starting to really understand what being an only parent was like. I dug a large bonfire pit in the back yard and laid a stone patio down around it, a larger version of the fire pit I'd had back in Bedal. The space had become a focal point of the gatherings we had multiple times a month.

It had been a week since the last get together and it hadn't taken much prodding to get Sienna to join everyone out back. I knew that in the past week she had been joining Avianna in the kitchen and they had been baking up a storm of sweets. I made a note that I should get Avianna something as thank you for extending an olive branch to the timid newcomer even after the comments made previously. I knew that many of those from the Westerguard clan, all of whom had been born shifters, sometimes didn't understand what those of us who survived attacks felt, especially in the beginning. I remembered all too clearly what it had been like learning that every month I would turn into the animal who had slaughtered my family.

Shaking the memory off, I brought the beer up to take another sip when I felt the tension rising around me. I downed the rest of the bottle in one swig just as I heard voices being raised behind me. With a weary sigh I set the now empty bottle on the ground and stood, ready to end whatever fight was brewing before it could really start. All I needed was for Sienna to see two of these idiots acting like animals to send her running back to the safety of solitude in her room. I rolled my neck and shoulders in case I needed to physically step in. Soon I was going to just start knocking heads together when the testosterone went into overdrive. I laughed a little at the thought, and here I was calling the others animals. To my surprise, instead of finding two Alpha's testing their strength, or the cat fight between two Omega's, I found Sienna cowering back from Mathias, one of my troubled Alphas. After the momentary shock I sighed in defeat, one of these days I knew I was going to have to put Mathias down, I was hoping today wasn't going to be that day. That's all I needed, the timid and damaged Omega to see me kill one of my own people. Maybe I would talk to Mark to see how he thought we should handle this problem. As I moved closer I was able to better make out the words he was spewing.

"Omega's like you are why the shifter community is going to hell," I felt my blood rage at his slurred words. Of course he was drunk, it always brought out his belligerent side. The fact that he was aiming that malice towards Sienna made my beast see red, maybe today would be the day we ended him after all. I would just need Avianna and Melody to take Sienna away first, "A knocked up, unmated Omega is nothing but a disgraced filthy whore." Watching the small dark woman flinch I had had enough. I stepped forward pushing Mathias back hard enough to send him stumbling and standing between them.

"That is enough" I let my voice bellow over the crowd. "I expect more from my people than to treat an outsider like this." I stood firm between the drunk Alpha and cowering Omega, "Not to mention Sienna isn't just an outsider, she is a guest in our home, in our lands. We do not treat guests like this. We do not judge those whose story we don't know; hell we don't judge anyone no matter their story. From now on Sienna is under my protection. Anyone who has a problem with that can challenge me themselves." I waited looking around the group, meeting each of their eyes, "Is that understood?" I put a little power behind my words and watched as all of my shifters lowered their gazes in subservience.

"Yes my King," were the resounding echoes back as they looked back up at me.

"The next time one of my pack shows disrespect to Sienna I will take it as a direct challenge to my position as Alpha, is that understood?" again I put as much authority as I could into the last word and again my shifters all dropped their gazes from mine.

"Yes my King," echoed back to me again. I dropped the gaze from the crowd, directing it instead at the drunken alpha in front of me. As my eyes met his I let them go cold, let him see how close he was to bringing on his own end.

"Mathias, get out of here, and this is your last warning about how we treat Omegas. If I ever hear you disrespecting an Omega again ever, whether they are part of this pack or not, you will be exiled." With a growl he turned and stormed off, "Dismissed." I turned to face Sienna, to make sure she was ok, only to see her storming off back towards the house. The sight stopped me in my tracks and for a moment I was seeing Raylene storming away from me after telling me off for some idiotic thing I had done wrong.

"Go after her," Melody said, suddenly appearing next to me, Aurora on her hip. Her voice pulled me from my memory.

"What?" I looked down at the Omega confused.

"Alaric, go after that girl and make sure she is ok," she laughed and shoved my shoulder, pushing me towards the house.

"I don't - "

She cut me off before I could finish, "Go." She said pointing a finger toward the house before turning and walking away talking to Aurora in the high pitched baby voice, "Sometimes your Uncle Ric Ric is a big dumb dumb, especially when it comes to pretty Omegas." I growled lightly and rolled my eyes before turning and making my way towards the house. I wandered through the house until I found Sienna in the kitchen angrily washing the dishes. I stood there for a moment unsure of how to approach this Sienna. I had gotten so used to approaching her while scared that seeing her angry rooted me to the spot.

I took a deep breath and decided to just approach her the same way I had been for the last several weeks, "Sienna, are you ok?" I kept my voice soft and stayed back from the timid Omega. I flinched as she slammed a pot down in the sink, water splashing up and over the sides, "You don't have to do that, we have people who do that." I knew it was stupid to focus on the fact that she was doing the dishes, but I was so far out of my element with this that it was the only thing I could think to do.

"I," she stopped and took a deep breath, her shoulders rounding before turning to face me. I took a step back when instead of her deep brown eyes being filled with fear they glinted in rage, "Why did you do that?"

"Do what?"

"Why did you step in between us?"

"Because that's my job as Alpha, as King. He was being an ass and I don't put up with my people acting like that or my people being treated like that." I took a deep breath and rubbed a hand across the back of my neck, "And I did it because you have been through enough, I won't let my pack put you through anymore."

"They won't respect me now. Not if they are tiptoeing around because they are afraid of you."

"I was protecting you, again that is my job as Alpha and King."

"You aren't my Alpha, like he pointed out. I don't have an Alpha." I could hear the scathing in her words.

I don't remember moving but I was suddenly in front of her, "I am your Alpha and I am your King, the same way that I am their Alpha and King," my voice dropped to a whisper "and I protect those in who are under my reign." I cupped her face in my hands and lowered my mouth to hers. The kiss was gentle and chaste but still firm and demanding. I refused to let up until I felt her relax into my arms. When I pulled back I let her curl into my arms and just held her close. My beast cheered inside of me and urged me to take her now, to make her ours. I ignored him and let myself luxuriate in the victory of her letting me comfort her.

Chapter 10

Sienna

It had been three days since Alaric had kissed me in the kitchen and I still wasn't sure how I felt about it. For the last three days we had done our best to avoid each other, and I had taken refuge in the library when not in my room. The longer I was here the more I fell in love with this room and I couldn't wait until the weather got cold enough to justify asking Alaric if I could start a fire in the red brick fireplace again. The bookcases that lined the two walls on either side of the wall that the door was on ran floor to ceiling and had one of the sliding ladders that I had to fight the urge to slide on like I was Belle in Beauty and the Beast. The shelves were a dark wood and filled with so many books I hadn't managed to even make a mental catalog of them. The center of the room held two dark brown leather love seats that faced each other with a matching couch that faced the fireplace. On the wall opposite the door held the red brick fireplace that was framed on either side with floor to ceiling windows that looked out over the rolling back yard. I had spent so many hours in this room that I was almost sure that I could have made my way through it with my eyes closed and never bumped into a thing. I had settled into one of the love seats, the faux fur blanket from my room draped over my legs when there was a soft knock on the double doors. I fought not to show how startled I was at the knock and took a moment to calm myself before seeing who was there. I looked up to see the small brunette from the first pack get together and I racked my brain for her name.

"Hey, Melody and I were thinking of heading out for lunch and wanted to know if you wanted to join us. Just a small girls day out." I chewed on my lip thinking over the invitation. I knew that Alaric wanted me to start getting to know the rest of the pack, and nodded slowly. I couldn't keep locking myself away in the house and this way it would be hopefully safe enough with the three of us.

"Yeah that sounds nice," I forced a smile on my face even as I fought to keep my breathing steady.

Her smile brightened the room, "Great, we will meet you out front in ten, will that give you enough time to get ready?"

I nodded, "Yeah that shouldn't be a problem." I didn't know how to tell her I didn't exactly have a whole lot of clothing options to choose from to go out to lunch with. I tucked the book I had been reading under my arm and headed upstairs. I dug through my bag and pulled out the nicest looking jeans I could find and a red silky feeling button up blouse. When

I tugged them on I knew I was going to have to find a way to get the next size up clothes soon as both were getting tight on my ever growing stomach. I grabbed my purse and sighed when I remembered that I had given the last of the money Alex had given me to the driver. I argued with myself a few moments before slipping downstairs and knocking hesitantly on the office door.

"Come in," the Alpha's voice called from inside. I slid into the room keeping my head ducked, eyes down cast, "Sienna," his voice sounded surprised, "What can I do for you?"

"I'm sorry to ask for anything else as you've already been so kind to me but a few of the Omegas asked me to go to lunch with them and I realized that I gave the last of my money to the driver who brought me here."

"It's no problem at all, you are a guest of the pack," I heard some rustling and the next thing I knew I was being handed a credit card, "use this for whatever you need."

I looked up at him in shock, "Alaric, I can't accept this."

He interrupted me before I could continue, "You can, and you will. You are a guest here and are in need of help, that is what a pack does for each other. Now, take the card, and go out to lunch with Avianna and Melody." I nodded numbly while also trying to remember the name of the two Omegas that he said.

"Alaric?" I paused in the doorway and looked back at him as he settled down behind the desk again. The thought of the kiss rearing its ugly head again.

"Hmm?" he barely glanced up and I felt my stomach plummet. Maybe I had been the one avoiding him since the kiss, maybe it hadn't meant a thing to him. Was a kiss like that just another difference between humans and shifters? I felt like I was never going to understand the rules of being a shifter.

"Thanks," I said instead of what I had been thinking.

***

I laughed softly at the small baby, Aurora, when she clapped happily as Melody moved the spoon of mashed potatoes towards her, "She's absolutely precious Melody," I smiled at the Omega on the other side of child, and I could easily see that she was on the path to look like her mother.

"Just wait, you will think the same about yours, until you have been up for a week straight" she grinned.

I smiled, "I helped with my niece and nephews when they were babies, I know what I'm in for."

"Does your family know you are ok?" Avianna asked.

I shook my head looking down at my plate, "No, I couldn't bring myself to call them once I knew what I was."

"Being a shifter isn't that bad." Melody's voice was soft, "I was born a shifter, so was Cal, and so was Aurora. We are just like humans, the only difference is that once a month we have to turn furry and we have some advantages even."

"Advantages?" I couldn't keep the doubt from my voice.

"We are faster, stronger, have better hearing and sight," Melody shrugged, "We can't catch most diseases and we age slower, thus we live longer than humans. "

"I didn't know any of that." I said softly. Did those advantages take away from turning into an animal, a beast, once a month?

"You were never taught," Aviana's voice was soft, "the rest of us were. We can teach you too, if you want to learn."

"Honestly I'm not sure. I know you guys are really nice, so is pretty much everyone in the pack, but I still feel like I'm a monster." I kept my voice low so no one at the surrounding tables could over hear me. "After what he did to me it's hard to reconcile with everyone here."

"Give it time, but know that you have people here who want to help you, who want to be your friend." Melody smiled just as Aurora started to cry, "I think we should get this little girl home before she has a meltdown and disturbs all the people here for high tea." We all stood and headed out to the car, stopping for Melody to pay the bill with the card Alaric had shoved at me as we headed out to lunch.

When we stepped outside I tipped my head back feeling a rumble in my throat as I felt the sun warming my face. I blinked over to the others eyes going wide, "Did I just, purr?"

Melody laughed a little, "That's what it sounded like. What do you turn into?"

"turn into?" I let the confusion I felt fill my voice.

"What is your animal form?" Avianna asked softly.

"A um, mountain lion?" I answered uncertainly. "Wait are there different types of animals?"

"Yes, most travel through the familial lines, though that has started to change as different animals have inter-mingled. We are still trying to figure out what side the offspring will take after in those cases. And if you turn into any form of a big cat then yes, you just purred, most shifters of the feline flavor can." Aviana smiled, "see, it's not all bad." They linked their arms through mine as we headed towards the big black SUV. Avianna and I opened the passenger side doors while Melody moved around to put the baby in behind the driver side. I was just about to close my door when I noticed the cream envelope tucked under the windshield wiper. Frowning, I leaned back out of the car and pulled it free. When I saw my name scrawled on the front of the envelope my heart stopped and I could feel myself start to tremble. Slowly I opened the envelope and pulled out a folded piece of paper.

'Until I have you back in my arms, take care of my precious bundle and my kitty'

"Sienna, what's wrong?" Melody said as she got into the car. Her voice sounded faint and distant as I looked down at the picture of myself naked in a rusted dog kennel that had fallen into my lap from the paper when I unfolded it. I couldn't stop the shaking as I curled into myself, huddling against the door. I shouldn't have left the house, the safety of the pack's strong hold.

"Melody, what's wrong?" I could hear Avianna's voice behind me and heard Melody swear next to me as she took the paper from my lap.

"Call Alaric, tell him we are on our way back and he needs to be there," Melody ordered as she pulled from the curb.

Chapter II

Alaric

I watched Sienna walk away and wanted to call her back. It had been a fight since the kiss three days ago not to wrap myself around her but I knew that if I did that I would scare her away. Instead I had kept myself close to the house in hopes that she would seek me out. Just then there was a knock on the office door.

"Come in" My response was automatic before I even knew who was there but then I caught her scent before I even looked up. She stood in the doorway, head bowed like always. I ached to see her eyes whenever she was like this. I wanted to see them gleam with the fire

I was sure they had once held. "Sienna," I fought to keep my breath from sounding as breathless as I felt seeing her there, "What can I do for you?"

"I'm sorry to ask for anything else as you've already been so kind to me but a few of the Omegas asked me to go to lunch with them and I realized that I gave the last of my money to the driver who brought me here." Her voice was so soft had I still been human I would have had to strain to hear it.

"It's no problem at all, you are a guest of the pack," I quickly pulled my wallet from my back pocket and removed one of the pack cards. I never worried about which one I grabbed knowing all of them were always fully paid off each month,, "use this for whatever you need."

When she stepped forward and saw what I was holding out her eyes widened in surprise, "Alaric, I can't accept this."

I cut her off before she could come up with any excuses not to take the card, "You can, and you will. You are a guest here and are in need of help, that is what a pack does for each other. Now, take the card, and go out to lunch with Avianna and Melody." she nodded and took the card I held out to her. I felt a small pang of disappointment when she did so without letting her fingers even brush mine.

"Alaric?" She called me name as I sat down and saw that I had a new email from one the packs accountants

"Hmm?" I answered, letting my eye quickly scan over what they had sent over and filing it away for when it was time to do the pack's taxes.

"Thanks," she mumbled and I looked up just in time to see her flee the doorway. I sat back with a sigh and rubbed my hand over my face before reopening the pages and pages of financial data.

***

I growled as I tried to focus on the numbers in front of me. Every time I looked at these damn figures my beast suddenly wanted to do anything else. I never understood how Raylene had done this so easily, and had actually enjoyed balancing everything out. With a defeated sigh I shot a quick text off to Cal begging for him to help me finish balancing the pack's books for the month. I even threw in an offer to take Aurora so he and Melody could get away for a weekend. While I waited for a response I opened up one of my saved links and started to browse for new tools for the shop. I wasn't surprised when instead of a response text there was a knock on the door. I looked up just as Cal walked in with a smirk. "Shut up and come help me with these damned things."

He laughed as he came over pulling a chair around with him, "You know all you have to do is ask and I'll just take over doing this for you."

"Does that mean you are letting me off the hook for that offer to take Aurora?"

"Oh no, the cost for this month is you taking the kid for a long weekend, four days, three nights minimum. After this month though I'll take over pro bono if you want."

The temptation was high, but immediately I felt guilty for even considering it, "No, if Ray could do this for everyone, so can I."

Cal sighed, "You have to stop beating your-self up over every little thing. Raylene didn't pick you because you could do everything she did, but because you were a good leader, and sometimes that means delegating to others."

I was thinking over this when Ryan burst into the room, his scent filled the office with his panic. "What's wrong?" I asked standing up, the pack's finances completely forgotten. If anything had happened to Avianna I would help him to bring the world down for her. And then I remembered, she was with Sienna, Melody and Aurora. That thought made me see red.

"Avianna called, I don't know what hap-pened but she said something was wrong with Sienna and that you needed to be out front waiting when they got back." he said meeting my eyes, "She sounded shaken up."

"What about Melody and Aurora?" Cal asked from next to me.

"I don't know, she just said that there was a note left for Sienna on the car, that they were on their way back and they needed Alaric to be waiting for them." With those words all three of us rushed from the room and the house to wait for the three Omegas to get back home.

***

I paced in front of the house waiting for the girls to get back from their day out. It had only been ten minutes since Ryan had burst into my office and I knew that all of their favorite restaurants were at least a twenty minute drive from the house. Even knowing that I couldn't bring myself to be calm or patient. I should have never let them leave without protection but I had let Melody guilt me into it using the interaction the weekend before with Mathias. I wouldn't allow it again. Until whoever this monster was was caught no Omega close to me would leave without an Alpha escort. It was going to raise hell with several of the more pig headed ones, but they would get over it. My blood had turned cold when Ryan had given me Avianna's message though and I wouldn't put anyone else at risk. If any of the four girls were hurt I would burn the world down around whoever had caused it. As soon as Melody pulled through the gate I was at her door.

"Let me see it," I growled out the order. Melody closed the door behind her as she slid out of the truck and handed me an envelope. As soon as she handed it to me Cal was pulling her into his arms, his hands skimming over her to make sure she was ok even as she quietly assured him that she was. I looked down at the envelope she had given me, Sienna's name scrawled across the front. I pulled out the folded paper inside and read the words on the page, but when I saw the picture that was tucked within my blood boiled. "Where were you guys," I demanded, shoving the papers back into the envelope and shoving all of them into my back pocket. I had to get myself together before I went to pull Sienna from the car or I would undo the little bit of trust I had earned.

"Alaric, you need to calm down. She needs reassurance right now." Melody said her voice low and even from where she was held within Cal's arms, their small daughter cradled between them both, "if you approach her like this you will terrify her."

It was as if she were echoing the words in my head but still they triggered something inside of me, "I would never hurt her. I would never hurt any of you, or anyone in my pack."

"I know that, and you know that, and Avianna even knows that. Sienna, though, doesn't. She is used to being hurt by the Alpha in her life, so if you go to her in a rage she will recoil from you. She will no longer feel safe with you Alaric the way she has started to. When she saw that letter she," Melody shook her head, "it's like she disappeared within herself when she saw it, Alaric. I haven't been able to get any reaction from her since she saw that. Don't scare her anymore than she already is." She reached out to place her hand on my arm.

I closed my eyes and took a breath, steadying myself. I nodded and squeezed Melody's hand softly before pulling the envelope back out and handing it back to her, "Take that to Tanya, see if she can get it analyzed and get anything from it." She nodded and I walked around the truck to the passenger side door. I opened the doors, "Sienna," I said, working to keep my voice calm, "It's ok, you're home, you're safe." As soon as she heard my voice she launched herself into my arms. I caught her and held her to me. "You're ok now. You're safe," I soothed holding her close. I ran my hand over her short black hair and down her back as she sobbed and shook in my arms.

Suddenly I was outside of an old bar and another small woman was sobbing into my chest. My heart stopped and my breath caught as I remembered that first time I held Raylene to me. That first time she let herself be just her and not a Queen. I closed my eyes and lowered my face to her head, taking in her scent. The scent reminded me that I was not holding Raylene, that my mate was dead, but the Omega here needed me now. I hadn't been able to save Raylene, but I would save Sienna even if it was the last thing I did.

"He found me," her voice was a choked sob as she said the words over and over. I lifted her into my arms and cradled her against me. I nodded towards Cal and Ryan to take care of their mates and carried the trembling woman into the house. I bypassed the couple of pack members who had filled the entryway and moved straight to her room.

Chapter 12

Sienna

I heard doors opening and voices filtering in from outside but couldn't bring myself to care, he had found me. When my door opened I could sense Alpha and jerked back looking up as I tried to scramble away but the seatbelt held me in place. It wasn't until my eyes locked on Alaric's own panicked green ones that I reversed my path and in that moment all I wanted was to be in his arms. I wanted to feel safe the way I did every time I let myself be wrapped in his arms, "Sienna," Alaric's voice was soft and soothing, "It's ok, you're home, you're safe."

My fingers clawed at the seatbelt trying to release it. When I finally heard the click I threw it off and launched myself into him, wrapping myself around him as tightly as I could. I clung to him as I finally gave into the panic and began to cry and shake, "He found me, he found me," were the only words I could say through the tears and I said them over and over again.

I held onto him as he shifted me so he could cradle me in his arms and carry me inside. He paused at the top of the porch steps and I heard him murmur to whoever was there with him before he continued through the house. Hearing a door open and close I blinked up and saw he'd brought me to my room. Tucking myself into his chest again, I could feel him walk across the room and sitting in one of the chairs near the window.. He was running his strong, slightly rough hands soothingly over my back using a soft voice that would normally be used to comfort a scared or crying child. The terror flowing through me at seeing the letter resulted in an adrenaline crash in Alaric's arms, carrying me into an exhausted state of sleep, my hands still clutching his shirt like a lifeline.

***

I woke to the evening sun warm and bright across my face, and my head resting on a hard chest instead of the pillows I was used to. I looked up to see Alaric's face, slack in sleep. His head was tilted back to rest on the back of the chair, both his arms were wrapped around me gently. Slowly I pulled myself free from his arms and slipped from his lap. I stood looking down at him and watched him frown in his sleep, waiting until his face relaxed again before heading towards the bathroom. Stopping at the closet I grabbed a pair of stretchy pajama pants and a large t-shirt, bringing them into the bathroom with me. I set the clothes on the counter and paused for a moment, this is where I would normally grab the gold knife from under the mattress and drag in the chair, but then I saw Alaric sleeping in the chair and I knew that no one would get past him into the bathroom. Forcing myself to stay calm I closed and locked the door behind me before getting in the shower and turning on the spray. Even under the steaming water I couldn't relax fully, my muscles stayed tight and tense as if I were prepared to run, to fight and I guess I was. I was ready to flee from this place that only twenty-four hours ago was a safe haven for me, and at the same time I was so tired of running. I was tired of running, of being scared. I liked being here, and at that moment I promised myself that I would stop being so scared and that I would fight for the life I had started to build there. After several minutes of trying to let the hot water soothe me, I gave up and washed quickly before getting out. I toweled my hair dry and ran my fingers through it. I couldn't stop the memory of the night he had hacked my hair off from flooding back.

I was kneeling on the floor of the base-ment, my heart pounding. He only brought me down here when things would get messy. Maybe this was it, maybe he was finally going to kill me. I wanted to huddle around myself to protect myself but I knew that would only make whatever he was planning worse. Suddenly I felt his fingers tangling in my hair yanking back. my scalp screamed as I arched back to try to relieve the tension but he kept pulling until I couldn't bend back any more. I whimpered, feeling my breath speeding up, I was on the verge of hyperventilating. He snarled in my face and I saw the flash of a blade. This was it, he was going to finally kill me. I closed my eyes expecting to feel the sharp sting across my throat. When instead I felt the jerking motion of the knife as he hacked and sawed at my hair, I gasped. The rancid smell of his breath invaded my senses as he whispered in my ear that if I didn't learn to behave my hair wouldn't be the last thing his blade saw.

I jerked back to the present at the hard knocks on the door. I stumbled back and had to catch myself on the sink while I tried to catch my breath. So much for not being scared and fighting.

"Sienna, are you ok?" Alaric's voice came through barely muffled, "Sienna, I need you to let me in. Please. I can feel your fear, I need you to let me in or to at least tell me you are ok."

"O-One minute" I called back and quickly pulled the clothes I had grabbed on before opening the door. I found myself looking directly at Alaric's chest. When I looked up into his compassion filled green eyes, I saw concern, but only for a second because then he was pulling me against him, into the safety of his arms again.

"I felt your distress, you are safe here Sienna." His voice was softer. I nodded slowly and stepped back from him.

"I'm ok, It was a flashback is all. It was a memory from when I was with him." I hugged myself, "I don't want to ever be at his mercy again Alaric."

"You won't be, he won't touch you Sienna." I nodded and walked around him to sit in the chair opposite the one we had slept in. He sat down back in the same chair facing me.

"Promise me?"

"I promise." We sat in silence for a moment, "Tell me what I can do to help."

"Distract me, Please." I whispered looking out the window.

"Tell me how and I will. Tell me what I can do to distract you."

"Tell me something about yourself. I heard you were changed like I was, that you aren't a born shifter," I turned to look at him and changed my request when I saw the pain on his face, "How do you get over not being human anymore?"

"That's not what you were going to ask." He said softly, "You wanted to know about my human life." All I could do was nod. He took a deep breath and started talking. I leaned my head against the arm of the chair and listened as he talked about his wife, about finding out they were expecting a baby. About being a dad, about life with his family. When he started to tell the story about his transformation I moved back to curl up in his lap, giving both of us the comfort of touch that we needed.

Chapter 13

Alaric

I sighed, what was it with these women always wanting to know about the past? What was worse was the fact that I could never tell them no. I took a deep breath and began to tell her my story. I told her about meeting Kate in high school, about how I'd had to practically beg her to go on a date with me. I told her the story about how I had fumble proposing to Kate and then about what it had felt like seeing her walking down the aisle. I relived first the birth of my son, my mini me, and then of my baby girl. When I got to losing them and being turned I had to pause and swallow back the tears. Just as the feelings of the past began to overwhelm me, she closed the distance between us and curled into my lap again. And just like that everything inside me calmed again. After a few hesitant moments I let my hand fall to her hair, fingers combing through the short silky strands. I closed my eyes as I skipped the rest of my transformation and instead began to relive the beginning of my life as a shifter. I told her about meeting Cali-Ann, and challenging their old Alpha, about the several years I spent so deep in the bottle I could barely see straight and Cali-Ann had to drag me home or to my shop every night. I didn't shy away from the period when I felt as she did, that I was a monster. This was a part of my story that only those who lived it with me knew about. I had never told Raylene that I had spent years believing I was a monster. Not to the degree I explained it to Sienna. When I got to that first meeting with Raylene I paused and looked down. Seeing Sienna asleep again I let my story end, not yet ready to relive the year before.

Standing up I cradled her to my chest as I moved to the bed. She was small enough that I was able to hold her one handed as I reached down to pull back the covers before laying her gently on the bed and pulled the blanket up to her shoulders. As I did I noticed for the first time that her hair didn't look like it had been cut evenly. Looking closer, it almost seemed as if someone had hacked at it with a dull blade. Just the thought of the faceless monster doing something so cruel made my vision start to go red. Taking a few calming breaths I made a note to talk to Melody to see if we could arrange a spa day for Sienna, one in the house. Before leaving I made sure the lamp on the nightstand was on, the same as she slept every night. The setting sun may be providing ample light now, but I knew within the hour the room would be plunged into darkness.

As I jogged down the stairs I sent off a text to Cal, Mark, Cali-Ann and Alana to meet me in the office immediately, then I sent one off to ask Melody to stop by when she had a free moment. While waiting for them I pulled up the pack registry and searched for the contact information for the pack Sienna had mentioned when she first came here.

"Hey, how is Sienna?" Melody asked softly from the door. I shouldn't have been surprised that she would have stopped in before the others arrived.

"She's sleeping," I sighed and scrubbed a hand over my face, "This morning really shook her up."

Melody nodded, "I had noticed. So what did you want to ask me?"

"I noticed that it looks like someone hacked at Sienna's hair. I don't think she will let me pay to send her to a salon, but maybe if it was a group event that was brought to her she would agree. I thought maybe if you could bring someone in to give her a full spa day and not just her. You and Avianna should join her too, she seems to have started trusting the two of you. I don't want her to have to leave the house again until she is ready but I think maybe the full works: hair, nails, facial and massage. Do you know people that we could trust to bring in?"

Melody smiles, "Yeah I'll take care of it, how about this weekend? I know a few people who owe me big that I can call in for this."

I smiled, "That sounds perfect, thank you Melody." I watched her walk away just as Cali-Ann strolled into the office.

"What's up boss?" she asked, dropping into a chair across from me, legs hanging over the arm as she draped her arms over the back.

"Wait for the others." I ordered as I quickly sent off a short email to the Alpha of the other pack who first rescued Sienna. I ignored Clai-Ann's raised eyebrow. None of my pack were used to me giving such short and harsh orders, especially not Cali-Ann who had been by my side from the moment I had stepped into Bedal all those years ago. It took only a few more tension filled minutes before the others filed into the office, Mark closing the door behind him.

"Gonna tell us why you called us here now?" Cali-Ann said, her voice tinged with a challenge. I closed my eyes and forced myself to chill the fuck out. They didn't deserve for me to take my anger at Sienna's tormentor out on them.

"We need to find out more about whoever it was who first changed Sienna." I said calmly and turned to look at them all. Taking another steadying breath I told them the story Sienna had told me. I felt bad betraying her trust by telling them her story, but I knew that it was what needed to be done. I would make it up to her somehow. When I finished I could feel the anger radiating off of each shifter in the room.

"I'll go to California and see what I can learn." Cali-Ann said, her voice low but even. It was a tone I only heard from her when she was on the verge of ripping someone's throat out, and I approved of that move in this case.

"I'll reach out to the other packs to see if any of them have any information." Mark said.

"On another note, while I agree we need to work on removing the threat, from what Melody told me it sounds like Sienna has no idea how to be a shifter. She needs to be taught how to take care of herself, to not be just his victim. We need to teach her how to use her animal and those heightened senses to protect herself, to defend herself." Cal said his voice soft.

I clenched my jaw but nodded, "I think it would be a good idea to have her start learning with Melody and Aviana. Sienna seems to feel safe around them. I know we would normally have a couple of the Alphas do this but Sienna isn't comfortable with men or Alphas. Cal, will you talk to Melody about setting some time aside? I know that you guys have Aurora, but I would really appreciate it."

"It's not a problem, I'll wrangle Ryan into helping with Aurora while our mates work with Sienna." Cal said, giving the other Alpha a light shove.

I nodded my thanks, "Now I originally told her she would need to petition the pack, but I'm overruling that. She is now a part of this pack, this family. Spread the word, and if anyone has a problem with it, you send them to me."

"I don't think anyone will question your decision," Ryan spoke up for the first time.

"Well not anyone with any intelligence," Cali-Ann snorted.

I rolled my eyes knowing what was coming, "alright, you guys all know what needs to be done, get out of my office." I ordered them out before Cali-Ann and Mark could begin the banter they seemed to enjoy so much.

"Mel and I were thinking of a small cookout, if you thought Sienna would be up to it." Cal said from the doorway.

"Who all were you looking to invite over?" Even though I lived here most of the time, I rarely limited who was allowed to come over.

This time though I wanted to make sure that Sienna wasn't too overwhelmed.

"Just us and the two of you, Maybe Avianna and Ryan if they stick around."

I thought it over for a minute, "Yeah I think that would be ok" I stood and walked around the deck, "I'll go check on her."

Chapter 14

Sienna

Leaning against the porch rail I laughed as I watched Aurora, in the form of a tiny fuzzy brown bear, chase a human Cal and Melody around the back yard. "I can't believe she can shift at will and so easily. She's such a tiny thing."

"We keep telling you, there are so many positives to being a shifter." Alaric said from next to me.

"I know, but I just don't know how to see that," I whispered, placing a hand over my stomach. At nearly six months along, there was no denying that I was pregnant, "There's no way extra shifting can be safe for the baby."

"There are things you can do without shifting," his voice was soft, "Do you want to see?"

I looked down, thinking over his words, "I don't know."

"Do you trust me?" His voice was soft.

I jerked, looking up at him, "I do. I don't know why I do, I barely know you, but I trust you Alaric." He turned me back to face the yard and stepped up behind me, pressing himself lightly against my back.

"Close your eyes," He commanded gently. I leaned back into him just a little more, doing as he said, the sun bright behind my lids. "Now listen. Tell me what you hear." I strained to hear everything, or anything really, "relax, don't force it. Just relax and listen, let what comes come. You have the ability, you just have to learn to open it." His voice was barely above a whisper. I took a deep breath forcing myself to relax as I exhaled. Again I breathed deep, this time when I exhaled I could hear the faint rustling of grass as if something was moving through it. The faint thuds of paws hitting dirt. I was hearing the small family chasing each other in the yard. Not their laughs but I was hearing the shuffling of their feet along the grass.. I felt a smile stretching my lips and took another deep breath, pushing out my sense of hearing listening out farther from just the backyard. As I did I could hear the leaves rustling gently moments before I felt wind lifting my hair around my face.

I opened my eyes and laughed looking up at Alaric, "Can I do that all the time?"

He chuckled, grinning down at me and nodded, "with a little practice yes. You turn into a cougar. You have all of the advanced senses, even in human form. You just have to learn how to use them." I let myself lean into him fully as we went back to watching the three shifters bounding around the yard. After a few minutes he squeezed my shoulders gently before heading over to join Cal as he moved away from his girls and towards the grill. I took a few steps back and curled myself into a chair letting my mind wander over what Alaric said.

"You ok?" Melody asked, sitting down next to me and setting Aurora, who was now back to her human form, on the floor.

"I don't really know. My life has changed so much in the last year, I don't know how to handle it." I looked over at her, "I never used to be scared. But now? I swear the only time that I'm not afraid is when I'm near Alaric. Which is crazy because I barely know him and not to mention that he is a male, an Alpha. On top of all of that half the time he seems distant and almost cold."

"Alaric has been through a lot." Melody watched the baby while she played at our feet, "I know you've heard the name Raylene since you came here last month. She was my best friend my entire life, she was also our Queen, and she was Alaric's mate." I could hear Melody taking a deep breath and blowing it out, "We had a few traitors in the pack. They didn't like that Raylene was a Beta, and tried to kill Alaric." Her voice had gone soft, and I could hear the tears in it, "Ray pushed Alaric out of the way and took the gold blade meant for him. She wasn't the first person that Alaric loved who died."

"He told me about his wife and kids." I answered softly.

"Then you understand why he tries to distance himself from everyone," she took my hand and squeezed it soft, "Please don't take it personally."

I smiled back at her and squeezed her hand back, "You are a good friend, Raylene was lucky to have friends like you."

"We were lucky to have her."

"Can I ask a question though?"

"Of course."

"You said that she was a Beta, what does that mean? I've had Alpha and Omega explained to me, though since coming here it seems everything I was told before isn't exactly the truth, so maybe I really don't know anything."

"So Beta's are neither Alpha or Omega. It means that they feel the need to make the Alpha's happy like an Omega, but it also means that they want to protect the Omega's like an Alpha."

"Why would that be a bad thing?"

"Because it also means that they are sterile. Raylene would never have been able to give Alaric a pup."

"I still don't understand why that would make other people dislike her to the point of wanting to kill her."

"Had she not been our Queen, our leader, it wouldn't have been seen as big of a deal, but she was. And there is some ancient magic that works with our shifting that means that if a Beta is the leader of a group of shifters her infertility passed onto the people she governed. That's why she merged our clan with Alaric's pack." Just as she finished speaking Aurora started to fuss, "I think this little girl needs a diaper change." She smiled apologetically and stood picking the baby up and walking into the house, ending the conversation. "Hey Sienna?" Melody paused in the door with the fussy baby.

"Yeah?"

"Alaric asked me to set up a at home spa day for us, are you interested in that?"

"That sounds great, thank you."

***

A few days later I was sitting on the back deck with Aviana and Melody, our feet soaking in tubs of hot water, our hair wrapped in steamed towels.

"Is this what a spa day is like?" I asked, looking at the other Omegas.

"Kinda depends on what all you order and where you go. I figured we would keep it simple this time, just to kinda help us all relax after everything that happened."

I looked down, shame and guilt rushing over me, "I'm sorry for that."

"What happened wasn't your fault. Nothing that has happened to you at the hands of that maniac is your fault." I looked up at Melody.

"Did Alaric tell you what happened?" I couldn't stop the feeling of betrayal that filled me.

"No," she assured, reaching over to grab my hand, "I don't know your story Sienna, but I can guess parts of it. I didn't grow up with any attack survivors, my entire clan was made up of people born as shifters, but after the merge I have made friends with many survivors. I've noticed that many of the shifters who were attacked in more than one way tend to be more skittish. You don't have to feel pressured to tell me or anyone else in the pack anything, but know that if you ever need someone to just listen that I'm here for you."

"We are both here for you," Avianna said, giving my hand a squeeze. I didn't consider that there were so many shifters in this pack who were changed, and may have had a traumatic transition as Alaric and I did. Before I could respond the ladies who had been working on us came back out. They each set up a station at our right hands and started on the manicures. As I watched the one working on me brush on the pale pink polish onto my nails I couldn't help but wonder what would happen to the polish when I shifted in just a few days. The image of a mountain line with pale pink claws had laughter bubbling up my throat. When the others looked at me curiously I told them the thought that had popped into my head. Soon all six of us, the beauticians included, were laughing so hard that tears leaked from our eyes. At that moment I remembered how good it felt to laugh, I remembered what a day with my girlfriends back home had been like, and a small piece of me seemed to click back into place.

Chapter 15

Alaric

"Are you ready?" I asked looking down at Sienna where she stood in front of me. We were standing out in the backyard about ten yards from the edge of the woods. She returned my look nervously. I smiled and stepped closer to her. It had only been a few days of working with her but we were only two nights from the full moon where all of our abilities were at their highest, "You will do fine, once you start using your abilities they will become like second nature for you."

She closed her eyes and nodded, "I'm ready."

I smiled at the look of determination on her face. Gently I turned her to face the woods and gave a short whistle to those hiding in the woods, letting them know it was game time. "Don't open your eyes yet, use your nose, reach out with smell and see if you can tell me how many of them are hiding out there." I stepped back so that my own scent didn't interfere. I watched her lift her face to the wind and take a tentative sniff. Her nose crinkled as she started to take another breath, seeking out each scent.

"I think there are six pack members out there, but there are so many different animals, I can't count them all."

"For now focus on the pack members, use their individual smells and sounds and find them in the trees, tell me what colors they are wearing." She opened her eyes and peered into the woods. Before she could say anything I added, "You know all of the members that are in the woods, I want you to match name to scent and color." She looked hesitantly up at me but I nodded back towards the woods. She took a determined breath and looked back to the woods. I sat back and watched her scent and peer into the woods. It took her a few more minutes but she began to list off names and colors.

"Avianna is the farthest to the left in purple, and Ryan is next to her in green, he's a lot harder to see. Isn't wearing green in the woods cheating?" She asked, looking back at me.

I grinned, "Keep going, you can yell at Ryan for his color choice later."

She took another sniff, "Mel is in yellow, Cal in Red, and they have little Aurora between them in Orange." She looked back to me, her eyes weary, "I'm sorry but I dont know whose in blue to the right."

I smiled and gave a sharp whistle for everyone to come out, "You did good. One of my enforcers Alana was in blue, you've met her but only in passing."

Avianna came running up to the porch and pulled Sienna into a hug, "Don't listen to him, you did more than good, you did amazing. You keep practicing and you will be the best of us all." I laughed at the two and shook my head.

"You need to tell your mate that it's cheating to wear green for hide and sniff in the woods." Sienna smiled and hugged her back. It warmed my heart to see the easy affection between the two.

"I needed some advantage over the new super shifter," Ryan said from the other side of Avianna, sending his mate a wink.

"I think it is time for all of us to head in for dinner." Mel said with a soft smile before herding all of us inside, the baby on her hip.

***

After dinner I excused myself and headed down to the office. It had been one of the best days I'd had since losing Raylene, and definitely the best day I'd had since Sienna had knocked on the front door. I knew I should have been happy but my thoughts wouldn't stop swirling and I needed to go someplace to calm myself. I sat behind the large desk in the office and looked at the picture of Raylene on her graduation day. I knew that Melody had a similar picture, but it was her and Raylene in their matching graduate robes hugging each other. Back then Raylene had worn her white hair long and it had hung loose to her mid back. By the time I had met her, her bright teal blue eyes had lost a little of their sparkle, faded by the burden of duty her fathers death had dropped on her shoulders. She had cut her hair to shoulder length and rarely wore it loose. I looked back at the picture, she smiled brightly at the camera with her fathers arm around her shoulders hugging her close. After she died I couldn't bring myself to remove any of the personal items she had had in this office and I closed off her bedroom. When I let Cal and Melody talk me into moving into the huge house I had opted to move into the room that had once belonged to her parents.

"Hey you ok?" I looked up to see Cal in the doorway.

I laughed a little and shrugged, "Truthfully I have no clue. What does ok even feel like?" He stepped in and closed the door behind him.

"How about a drink?" he said walking over to the small bar in the corner, it was one of the few changes I had made to the room. If I was going to have to balance numbers I needed alcohol at the ready.

"Honestly, I could probably use one." I watched him pull a bottle of scotch from the cabinet and poured us each a glass. He handed one to me before he sat down across the desk from me.

"Why don't you tell me what's going on."

"I don't know man. I can't seem to wrap my head around everything. It's like the world won't stop throwing me curve balls. I can't seem to get my balance," I took a deep breath, and downed the entire glass in one gulp relishing in the burn of the liquid down my throat, "I care for her, more than just as her King."

"Sienna?" I nodded, "Have you talked to her?"

"What is there to talk to her about? She's broken Cal, and I am not the person who should be fixing anyone, especially someone as delicate as she is. She deserves someone who will give her their all, not someone who's still in love with not one but two other women, both of whom are dead. She needs someone who can protect her and I don't exactly have the best track record in protecting the women I love."

"I won't tell you to let them go, I know that if anything were to ever happen to Melody or Aurora I would never be able to forget them, to love them less. What I will tell you is that you deserve to be happy Alaric. You have done so much for all of your people, and Raylene's. I know that you feel you should have protected her but she felt the same way. That's why she pushed you out of the way that day. She knew what she was doing when she stepped in front of that blade. How do you think she would have felt if you had been the one who died? She didn't take that blade just for you, but for all of us. Raylene did her research, she knew that you were the best possible person to hand her people over, and that's what she was doing when she sacrificed herself. If you let yourself grow cold and distant, which you will if you can't learn to open up to someone new, then you will fail her worse than if you had died with her."

"How can I take another mate after Ray? Another wife after Kate? I reasoned with myself that what me and Ray had was different from what I had with Kate. I thought because she was my mate and not my wife I wasn't betraying Kate's memory. Now though, Sienna deserves someone who can be her mate and her husband and I feel like giving her either is betraying one or both of them." I looked at my friend, "And then adding a baby on top of all of it. How could I ever give to another child what I gave to the two I couldn't keep safe? What if I can't keep this one safe? I don't know if I can handle any more loss Cal."

"It's not a betrayal Alaric. They both loved you and would want you to be happy. You also have to remember that anyone you choose, whether it be Sienna or someone else, will also have the protection of the pack behind them. It won't be the same as with Raylene, we will watch your back, their backs, and that includes any children you do or don't have. I know Raylene for sure would want you to find someone who made you happy. She wouldn't want you to lock yourself away and suffer for the rest of your life because of her sacrifice." He set his now empty glass on the desk and stood, "Just remember, she didn't die so that you could be miserable. She died so that you could live, and loving is part of living." He reached across and squeezed my shoulder before heading for the door.

I picked up the picture of Raylene, taken years before I ever met her and turned to look out the big window over the dark yard. Out in that yard lay the woman I love, next to her parents in the pack's cemetery, "How am I

supposed to do all this without you Princess?"
I whispered and closed my eyes.

Chapter 16

Sienna

The day after the full moon Alaric had given me the pack's credit card again and had insisted I go out with Melody and Avianna to purchase everything needed for the baby's nursery. He told me that I could pick out any of the rooms to turn into a nursery and that he would help me get everything set up. At first I had balked at the idea of leaving the house and had even asked him if he would come with me. I could see that as soon as I asked he wanted to say yes but instead told me that he had business to take care of. He asked if I would be ok with him sending Cal and Ryan as escorts instead. It had taken me a few minutes to think through if I would be comfortable with the two of them there but I remembered one of the nights before when we had all had dinner and realized that I had started to feel safe with the other two Alphas almost the same way I did around Alaric. After that realization I agreed that would be ok.

Both Avianna and Melody had been nearly giddy at the idea of baby shopping, and their enthusiasm was contagious. As we entered the store both Alphas opted to stay outside to keep an eye on everything, or so they said. I had a feeling that neither man was too thrilled with the idea of baby shopping. It didn't take too long for the cart to quickly fill up, not to mention the registration gun that Sienna had insisted we get.We had only made it to the bedding section, both Melody and Avianna scanning things like crazy. I ran my fingers over another soft blanket and resisted adding it to the cart.

"If you like it, get it," Avianna said with a smile.

"I already have like six blankets in the cart," I laughed, "It's just that they are all so soft, I want to just wrap myself up in them and never come out."

"Do you know what you want your nursery theme to be?" Melody asked as she dropped several thinner blankets into the cart, "Trust me you will need these."

I smiled at her, "Thanks, and honestly I have no idea what theme to do. I don't even know if I'm having a boy or a girl, how can I pick out a theme?"

"You could choose something gender neutral," Avianna suggested, "Like the night sky, or the ever popular zoo animals."

I made a face and laughed, "I don't think zoo animals are the way to go, but speaking of going I think I am going to make my escape to the restroom."

"We will continue to grab the essentials for you while you do that," Melody grinned in understanding. I nodded my appreciation before making my way through the store to the front where I had scoped out the restrooms as we came in. "Unless you want one of us or both of us to come with you."

I knew why she was asking. This was the third attempt we had made to go baby shopping but the last two times I hadn't been able to get out of the car. "I think I can manage, but thank you," I smiled before making my way through the store to the bathrooms at the front.

***

With a sigh of relief I stepped out of the restroom, pausing to see if I could see the other two Omega's. I had only taken a few steps when a hand wrapped around my arm gripping tightly just as I felt something sharp touch just above my jeans at my hip.

"Make even the smallest noise bitch and I'll cripple you." He hissed into my ear. And just the sound of his voice sent me flashing back. I whimpered and tried to pull away from his hand, "I see I am going to have to teach you about obedience again." He said, dragging me towards the door, I could feel my arm bruising under his grip.

"And we will be teaching you about keeping your hands to yourself," Ryan growled as we stepped outside.

"Mind your business" Kevin snapped, digging the tip of the knife in. I couldn't stop the whimper as I felt my skin split, hot blood seeping out to soak into the top of the jeans.

"She is our business," I heard Cal's voice from behind me even as I felt Kevin's pulse speed up where his fingers were digging into my arm, "Now I suggest you take your hands off of our pack member before we remove your hands all together." I screamed as I was shoved forward, Ryan catching me before I could fall. I heard the sound of a scuffle behind me before the sound of quickly retreating steps. I turned and saw Cal getting to his feet, a large gash across his chest.

"Cal," I screamed and rushed to his side. How could I tell Melody that her mate and her daughter's father was dead because of me?

"Ryan, go get the girls, get them checked out and to the car now," Cal ordered through gritted teeth, "Sienna, you need to get into the car now. We will lock the doors and wait."

"You're hurt, we need to call 911." I admonished trying to push him back down so I could put pressure on his wound.

"I'll be ok, we do need to get home and have Cora pack both our wounds, he had a gold blade and you are bleeding too. So please, just listen to me and get in the car." I couldn't stop myself from flinching back from the harshness in his voice but moved away from him and quickly to the SUV. I opened the door, silently insisting he get in first, before getting in after him.

I closed and locked the door before grabbing one of the multiple blankets from the previous store and ripping it open. Pushing through my fear I moved closer to him, "Let me put pressure on that." I kept my voice even and as calm as possible, ignoring my speeding pulse and impending panic attack. I waited for his nod before pressing the cloth to his chest. No matter how much I tried to stay calm I couldn't stop the whimper of fear when he growled from the pain.

"I won't hurt you, no one here would ever hurt you Sienna," his voice was strained and I nodded my head trying to blink back the tears.

"I know that, but my brain doesn't always want to listen when I tell it that." I whispered. I hated the fear I felt for someone who had just gotten hurt defending me. I closed my eyes and focused on slowing my breathing as I pushed down on his chest.

It seemed to take forever but eventually the back hatch opened as Avianna slipped into the driver seat and Melody climbed in next to Cal.

"I swear to God if you die on me Cal, I will kill you," Melody's voice was rough with tears.

"I'm ok baby, it's just a scratch," his voice was just as rough as before from the pain.

"I am so sorry," I whispered looking up at my new friend, eyes blurring with fresh tears, "I'm sorry for bringing this on you all. I'll leave, I'll go somewhere else."

"Stop it," Ryan snapped from the front seat as he pulled into traffic, and I huddled back against my door as far from him as I could get, "this is not your fault Sienna. This is the fault of a rogue shifter who is taking advantage of his abilities to torment those he should be protecting. While I can't speak for everyone in the pack, I can guarantee that Alaric will not let you go anywhere until we know that asshole has been caught." I watched through tears as Avianna reached out and squeezed his arm. I pulled my knees up as much as I could and curled myself into the corner of the seat while Melody took over holding pressure on the wound.

***

The drive was only about twenty minutes but in that time my anxiety skyrocketed and I had to push past several flashbacks of my time with Kevin. I wouldn't go back with him, I would rather die first. When we pulled up outside of the house Alaric and another shifter were waiting outside. As soon as the car stopped, before I knew what I was doing I had flung open the door and launched myself at Alaric. As soon as he wrapped his arms around me I felt something inside me settle and I felt the fear finally subsiding.

"It's ok Sienna, you're home, you're safe." He whispered against my hair.

"Please don't let him take me, please don't let him hurt me."

"I won't. I will take care of you." I felt him lift me into his arms and carry me into the house. "We need to have Cora take a look at this cut on your back. If it didn't heal on the way home then it needs to be tended to." I nodded against his chest.

"What's wrong with her?" a female voice sounded from inside the room.

"Cal said it was a gold blade, I don't know how deep it is." Alaric said.

"Lay her on her side and let me take a look."

I clung to Alaric as he tried to lay me down, "It's ok Sienna, I'm not going anywhere. I just need to lay you down so that Cora can take a look at that cut." I nodded and slowly loosened my grip on him. When he knelt on the floor near my head I felt something relax inside of me, until I felt fingers on my back near where Kevin and nicked me with the blade.

"Easy Sienna, I'm just checking to see how deep this is," The woman's voice was calm as she spoke, "It doesn't look very deep or long. I'm going to clean it up and add on a small poultice under a bandage. You should be fine by morning." I nodded my understanding but just kept my eyes locked on Alaric's. When I felt the cool wetness of a wipe on my back I squeezed my hand in his moments before I felt the burning sting of whatever they were using on the cut. It only lasted a few seconds and then she was smearing something thick and cool over the small section of my back. The goop was followed up with the feeling of what I assumed was gauze being taped down. "Everything is done. The bandage needs to be left on and kept dry for the next twelve hours, after that she can take it off and she should be completely healed."

"Thank you Cora." Alaric said as he stood again, "Do you want to walk up to your room or do you want me to carry you?" he asked in a gentle voice.

Before I could answer the woman, Cora I presumed cut in, "You should probably carry her unless you have a change of clothes for her. Where the cut is, her jeans are likely to rub the bandage off if she walks."

Alaric nodded before scooping me back up into his arms. I curled myself back into him. I buried my face against his chest when I heard voices outside of the door and didn't look up again until I heard the door of my room close behind us. He gently set me back on my feet but I couldn't bring myself to let him go. He ran a hand calmingly over my hair, "You are safe now, you are safe here."

Cautiously I tilted my head up to look at him. I felt my breath catch when the hand that had been soothing my hair moved to cup my jaw, his touch gentler than I had become accustomed to during the year of captivity I had suffered through. Despite the whisper of fear in the back of my mind I didn't stop him when he leaned his face toward mine. The kiss was as gentle as his hand was, and I let myself sink into him. I let myself feel safe in his arms, feel wanted by his touch. With a hand on my hip Alaric turned me and began walking backwards towards the bed, leading me to follow even while our mouths stayed connected. When he sat back on the bed, pulling his lips from mine, he gently pulled my top off. I felt heat rush to my cheeks and instinctively moved my arms to cover myself.

"Don't hide yourself, you are gorgeous Sienna," Alaric's voice was rougher than I could ever remember hearing it. He ran his hands up my sides and I let my head fall back at the feel of his warm rough palms on my skin. When he slid his hands back down I felt him grip my thighs, just below my ass, and he lifted me onto his lap. I shivered when he dragged his lips and then teeth along my throat before pulling off my bra and moving to my breasts. When his hot mouth wrapped around my nipple I cried out, hands gripping his shoulders even as my core clenched tight. Alaric chuckled as he pulled back and rubbed his stubble roughened chin along both breasts, "More sensitive than you are used to?"

I looked down at him panting and shook my head, "Never have been that sensitive before. Is it from being a shifter?"

He smiled and shook his head, chin rubbing against the sensitive skin again causing me to shudder in his arms, "No, this change is from being pregnant."

I blushed and looked down, "Does it bother you?" Before I realized what was happening he had lifted me and shifted us again, this time laying me back on the bed and hovering over me.

"There is nothing to be bothered by Sienna, unless you tell me no, I am very happy to be here." He waited, eyes on mine. I nodded slowly to let him know I was ok with what we were doing and my heart stuttered at his wolfish grin. When his mouth touched my skin again all thoughts fled from my mind. I lost track of time as he pulled noises from my throat I had never heard before. Only after he had covered every inch of me in a mix of butterfly kisses, soft nips, and the feel of his scruff scratching against my skin, did he push my legs open. Forgetting that we were not the only ones in the house I screamed in pure pleasure as he pushed two thick fingers into my weeping core, his mouth fastening over my throbbing clit. Over and over again he pushed me up and over that peak of pleasure, not stopping until I lay limp, whimpering softly.

I looked up at him through what looked like a haze when he moved over me. He leaned down pressing his mouth gently to mine, coaxing my lips open with his own. The kiss was slow and deep, stealing what little breath I had left. When he pulled back he lifted my hips and pushed a pillow under them, angling them up. I looked up at him, his eyes never left mine as he slowly pushed inside of me. I sighed, feeling myself stretching around him, hands scrambling at the bedding. Only when he was fully inside of me did he begin to slowly pull himself out of me, stopping with just the head of him still in me. Again he pushed forward slowly, filling me, my back bowing as pleasure flooded me. When he leaned over me and caught my overly sensitive nipple in his mouth again the world shattered around me.

When my mind righted again Alaric had re-situated us and had me curled into his side, a blanket pulled around me. I sighed out in content as I felt his hand stroking softly over my hair.

"Sleep Sienna, you're always safe here." I snuggled closer to him and felt his warmth and scent lull me to sleep.

Chapter 17

Alaric

I held Sienna tight to me as she slept. I wished I could call someone in to take her clothes out of the room. Even from on the bed I swore I could smell the reminisce of him on the fabric. When we first smelled him on her it had nearly driven my wolf into a frenzy. As we slowly covered every inch of her in soft kisses and slowly replaced his scent with ours, my beast calmed. In that moment we had started claiming her as ours. The urge I'd had to fight to stop myself from marking her, from fully claiming her had been the hardest fight I'd had with my beast for years. I held the sleeping Omega until I felt her body finally relax into that deep sleep. I held her as I dozed lightly, resting my cheek against the top of her head. When the sky outside her window started to lighten with the morning light I slipped from the bed. I turned on the lamp in case she woke before the room was bright enough and pulled my jeans on before leaving.

Exiting the room as silently as possible I sent Cal and Cali-Ann a message ordering everyone trained to be a bodyguard to report to my office immediately. As soon as the message went through I went to my room and changed into a set of fresh clothes. I contemplated a shower but couldn't bring myself to wash away the scent of her on my skin. Not while knowing the gravity of the decision I was making and knowing that it may be the last time I held her like that.

I paced along the office window while I waited for the others to arrive. I tried to calm the beast inside of me as I tried to calm my own tempest of emotions. He had almost taken her, we had almost lost her. We had almost lost another love. We could not protect those most important to us, we were not worthy of having a mate. I had to hold back a snarl when there was a knock on the door.

"Come in," my voice was still deeper than normal when I allowed them in.

"Are you ok my King?" Cal asked when he stepped inside ahead of the others. I closed my eyes and took a deep calming breath nodding. I was on edge and I knew the few I was inviting here would be able to tell. I had to get it together and fast.

"Yes, just bring everyone in," I said, moving to stand behind the desk as Cal opened the door farther to allow the others in.

"You requested us here Sir?" one of the Alphas asked once they all stood shoulder to shoulder along the far wall, bookended by Cal and the head of security Mark, who had been Raylene's head of security also.

"Yes. I'm sure you have all heard about the incident downtown yesterday." I let my eyes scan across the faces of everyone as they nodded. "We will not allow this monster to set hands on one of our pack again. I want one of you with her at all times if I am not, and there will be two guards on her whenever she leaves the grounds. If another non-guard pack member goes with her they will require a guard as well. The only place she will be allowed to go alone is into her suite, and even then one person will be outside of the door at all times. Am I understood?"

They all nodded and responded with a unified, "Yes Sir."

"My King, may I ask a question?" one of them asked, and I could hear the apprehension in his voice.

"Always." I nodded in encouragement.

"Do you plan to take Sienna as your mate?" I could feel the tension in the room thicken immediately.

I sighed and dropped into the office chair, slouching. I scrubbed a hand over my face as I tried to decide how to answer the question.

"At this time I have no intention to take her as a mate, I have no intention to take any one as a mate right now. I know that anyone I do choose to take as a mate will affect you as much as it will affect me. I want to assure you all that at this time I have no intentions to make anyone your Queen. I am asking you to protect her mostly because she deserves to feel safe after all she has gone through, not because I feel she deserves special treatment or because of my feelings for her. She has been here for nearly a month and while I know that she has not fully integrated herself into the pack I believe that she will make a good addition to the pack. We will never know though if we allow someone to hurt her, so please, help me protect her."

"Why don't you all go set a schedule, Cal and I will look it over." Mark ordered the others. We waited until they all had filed out and the door closed behind them before Cal and he took the two guest chairs opposite me.

"What's going on Ric?" Mark asked, keeping his voice soft.

I let my head fall back with a sigh, eyes closing, "I'm torn in so many directions right now."

"You and your wolf are fighting," Cal kept his voice as neutral as he could.

"Yes and no. We both agree on the fact that we are drawn to Sienna, and we both agree on the fact that we want to protect her. What we don't agree on is the best way to do that."

"How can we help?" Mark asked in his calm voice.

"I'm not sure you or anyone else can. The most you can do is to help me keep her safe. Make sure he doesn't get his hands on her again. And," I lowered my voice to just above a whisper, "help me find him. She will never be safe until he is dead."

"We can do that," Mark said and when our gazes met I could see the calculation in his dark brown eyes. "Once she's safe, will you allow yourself to be happy?"

"I can't take her as a mate," I shook my head, "she has been through too much, and being my mate would be too dangerous for her and for the little one she carries."

"Have you talked to her about it? Asked her what she wants?" Cal asked.

I shook my head again, "No, but I did tell her when she first arrived that she wouldn't be forced to mate with anyone."

"You wouldn't be forcing her. Everyone who is here often, since she has shown up, has seen the attraction between the two of you. And we all want you happy," Mark held up his hands before I could respond, "I understand your hesitation, but being near you is the safest place she can be."

"Raylene was right next to me when she was stabbed, being near me is what killed her." I snarled.

"This is different, you know that. Sienna isn't a helpless human like Kate nor is she as chivalrous as Raylene was. You cannot compare her to them. She is her own person, and

I think if you let yourself stop being afraid of loss, you could both heal together." With that he stood and left the room.

"He's right you know," Cal said watching me, "And we aren't saying this as your subjects who want a Queen, but as your friends who want you happy. I can't imagine the pain you have gone through, but I also can't imagine my life without Melody or Aurora. I also can't imagine the misery I would feel if I had to see her happy with someone else." And with that last statement he too left the office, closing the door to leave me alone with my thoughts.

Chapter 18

Sienna

I paced my room, an itch starting under my skin. It had been nearly two months since the incident at the store and I was feeling both smothered and completely alone. When I woke up the next morning I was disappointed to find that Alaric had left while I was still asleep. When I opened the door to find Mark the head of his security waiting for me I was confused. Both the disappointment and confusion took a back seat to rage when Mark informed me that per Alaric's orders I would be under 24/7 guard. The only time I was allowed to be unsupervised was when I was in my room. I immediately stormed to his office only to be informed that he had left for the weekend to handle matters at his shop in Bedal and would be back Monday for dinner.

Now two months later the inconvenience had turned into a burning annoyance. I was so tired of tripping over people I barely knew every time I turned around. Both Melody and Avianna had tried to console me that Alaric had only given the order to protect me after what had happened but what they didn't understand was that this was just another kind of cage and I was done being controlled. With a growl I stalked to the door and whipped it open to find one of the guards standing next to it in the hallway, Steve, I believed his name was.

"Did you need anything Miss Sienna?"

"Where's Alaric?" I couldn't even bring myself to get mad at the guards. None of this was their fault even if they did make handy targets.

"He had to go to his shop today. His majesty will be back before dinner." I wanted to roll my eyes. Dinner, that was the only time I seemed to see him anymore, "Is something wrong? Do you need me to call him?"

I shook my head, "No. I'm just going to head down to the library for a bit." I walked past him and made my way down the stairs, one hand resting on my stomach hoping it helped with my ever decreasing sense of balance. I tried to ignore the hulking shadow where he took up post at the door per usual as I started browsing the books that lined the walls. I had already read to the little one both of Lewis Carroll's Alice in Wonderland books, Peterpan, and the entire Winnie the Pooh collection. It took me a few minutes to find my next read but I quickly decided on Shakespeare and grabbed the complete collection in one book. I lowered myself onto one of the love seats, momentarily missing my ability to curl up like I had always loved doing. Taking a deep breath, I began to read aloud the beginning of King Henry the sixth. I wasn't sure how long I sat in the chair reading but I had made it through the entire play about King Henry the Sixth and the story of King Richard the Third before I closed the book and set it down on the small table. I rested my head back on the chair and closed my eyes.

"You read beautifully," the guard softly said from where he had taken up post near the door and I felt my cheeks heat up.

I shifted so I could face him over the back of the love seat, "Thank you, I used to volunteer at the local library reading to kids."

"You should talk with Melody, I'm sure she and some of the other pack moms would love to set something up with all the kids."

I smiled at him gratefully, "I will do that. Have you heard if dinner is ready?"

"I believe Avianna said that it would be done in about twenty minutes or so, are you ready to head to the dining room?"

"I think I'm going to lay down for a little bit," I fought back a yawn, "I may just ask to have dinner in my room tonight." I let him lead me back to my room, this time the thick book of Shakespeare tucked under my arm.

"Are you sure you are feeling ok? Nothing wrong with you or the little one?" he asked when we stopped outside my door.

"Just tired," I smiled up at him. "I'm pretty sure this is just normal pregnancy, but thank you for the concern."

"You have a good night Miss Sienna," he smiled down at me, "I will let them know that you have requested dinner in your room tonight."

"You too, and thank you." I closed the door and set the book on the nightstand. I changed into the loose tank top and shorts set before crawling into bed. I propped myself up with pillows and picked up the book to begin reading the next play, Tirtus Andronicus.

***

I groaned as I tried to shift, yawning as I did. I had fallen asleep while reading and now was stiff. Slowly I levered myself out of bed and swore as I waddled instead of walking towards the bathroom. Turning the shower on I stepped in letting the slowly heating water wake me up and work to loosen the muscles in my back. I missed the steaming hot showers that I had grown used to taking since I had arrived at the mansion but Cora had warned me of the dangers of hot showers so far into my pregnancy. With a sigh I ran a hand over my enlarged stomach.

"Ya know little one, you are already ruining my shower times." I smiled at the soft kick, "yeah we will have to just work through it won't we?" Stepping out of the shower I toweled off and pulled on a light blue sundress. Glancing in the mirror I grimaced, it didn't seem to matter what I wore nowadays I always seemed to resemble a beached whale. With a sigh I grabbed the book from the bed and headed towards the door. When I stepped into the hallway I couldn't stop the sigh of annoyance upon seeing the same guard outside of my room.

"Good morning Miss Sienna," he said with a smile.

"I know you guys are just doing what you were ordered, but I need some space, some alone time."

"You know that you are not to be disturbed when you are in your suite," he looked at me, eyes confused.

"I want to be able to move through the house without tripping over one of you, I want to go for a walk without feeling like I am being followed," I held up my hand, "I won't leave the grounds. There are nearly fifty shapeshifters here. I will be fine. I appreciate your guy's concern but I need space to breathe."

"The King won't like it."

"Then the King," I snarled, "can follow me around."

"He is at his shop in Bedal."

I ignored the sharp pain those words inflicted. Alaric seemed to be spending more and more time away from the rolling estate since our night together, "Of course he is. Well then you will just have to trust that I can take care of myself." I took a breath and tried to calm the rage I was feeling. Again this wasn't the guards fault, "I just need some time to be alone and enjoy fresh air."

"I don't think this is a good idea Miss Sienna." His brows furrowed in worry.

"Winter is almost here and then I won't be able to go outside. I want to go enjoy one of the last nice days of the year. I will even bring my blade with me, but I need some breathing room." With a weary sigh he nodded. I stepped back into the room and grabbed the gold blade from where it had been sitting on the dresser and strapped it around my thigh under the skirt of the dress. I walked out of the room and down the steps, my guard on my heels. When I got to the door to the three season room I turned and pointed at him, "Shoo now. I need some me time." I waited for him to move and sit at the table before I slipped from the house.

Stepping from the shadow of the house into the warmth of the sun. I tilted my face into the brightness, closed my eyes and took a deep breath and released the breath with a quiet purr. I hadn't been without someone next to me for nearly two months, and this one breath of fresh air felt amazing. I could feel the crisp coolness of winter in the air and knew I would miss this warmth soon. Keeping my face lifted to the sun, I walked along the back of the house towards the small garden I had been admiring from my bedroom window. I took another deep breath of the fall air, letting the mix of fragrances from the last blooming flowers fill my nose and lead me to the garden.

"Hello Sienna," the low voice made me jump just as my hand touched the gate of the garden. I turned, my heart racing to see Kevin standing at the corner of the garden, hidden by the side of the house.

"What are you doing here?" I hated that my voice shook as I stepped back from him.

"I came for my slut and my pup," his voice made me shiver in disgust.

"You need to leave. I am not yours. I never have been and never will be." I took a step back as he stepped towards me.

"You will always be mine." He rushed towards me. Before I could scream I felt the hard thud of his fist as it connected with my temple and a sharp pain at the back of my head before the world went black.

Chapter 19

Alaric

I rolled my neck as I pulled myself out from under a car. I had let myself get lazy staying at the estate all the time and my body was reminding me of how much harder working in the shop was. Despite the bits of pain I had realized how much I had been missing the work. I had missed being elbow deep in an engine compartment, getting my hands dirty.

"Are you still here?" Cali-Ann said and I looked up to see her perched on top of one of the tool boxes.

"I am going to change the keys to the shop and tell everyone not to give you a copy." I grumbled wiping my hands off on one of the shop rags.

"You know for the last year you have avoided this place and the memories it holds by hiding at the mansion. Now you are hiding here instead of facing your emotions for the Omega at the mansion. When are you going to stop hiding Ric?"

I let a growl trickle from my lips, "I'm not hiding, I'm working. You complained that I was ignoring my business well now I'm here and you accuse me of running from my feelings. You need to make up your mind Cali-Ann."

"Don't you go all Alpha on me Alaric," she snapped and I saw her eyes grow dark, "You don't get to be all pissy with me just because you don't like the truth that I'm telling you. There is a reason you keep me as your second and it's because I have never been afraid of you or of calling you on your bullshit. Stop running away from everything and man the fuck up. Go home, and make up with that girl."

"You are pushing it right now Cali-Ann."

"And you know I'm right." she shook her head, "I know that I'm not the first person to tell you this, I'm just the first person willing to keep pushing on it. I care about you Alaric, and I want you to be happy. I have always, and I mean always had your back from the moment we met. If I didn't think that this is what you wanted deep down then I would drop it, but I know you. Go get your happiness."

I slammed my hands on the top of the closed tool box and swore when I dented it. I let my head drop between my outstretched arms, "I don't know how to make it up to her. I ran after sleeping with her and haven't been around much since. I saddled her with bodyguards and from what Avianna and Melody have told me she is pissed about it."

"Start by getting rid of the babysitters, she isnt a child. After that apologize, let her smack you around some, because let's face it you deserve a few good smacks. Then tell her how you feel, if she feels about you the way you feel about her then she will listen." I thought about it for a moment and nodded, she was right.

"You are still a pain in my ass, you know that right?"

"And you wouldn't have me any other way," she said, hopping down from her perch and slipping an arm into mine. "Now let's get you out of here so you can go get your girl." She grinned as she pulled me from the shop.

***

I parked my bike in front of the large garage and wiped my hands over my face. I scrubbed a hand over my face and wondered how in the world I was going to make the last two months up to Sienna. For a moment I wondered if I should have stopped and picked up flowers. I shrugged it was too late now, maybe if she didn't talk to me tonight after I apologized I would stop and grab some tomorrow. Swinging my leg over the bike I balanced the helmet on the handle before heading towards the house, shifting my thoughts to the waiting hot shower. I could have showered at the shop like I used to, but part of me always felt an urge to get home as soon as I could so I was within reach of Sienna. Part of me wanted to go to her first, but in the back of my head I heard every female I'd ever had in my life telling me that one does not beg for forgiveness covered in dirt and grease, so shower first it was.

Opening the front door the shower was forgotten as I was hit with waves of panic and anxiety. Immediately I was on high alert. I moved deeper into the house, following the scent of fear. Each step I made had my muscles tightening, ready for a fight. Entering the kitchen, the emotions washed over me stronger than ever.

"What is going on?" I demanded, my eyes quickly moving along the shifters in the room. My heart stopped. Sienna was not one of them, yet all of the guards were there.

"My King," Steve, one of the newest guards, dropped to his knees in front of me, "Please forgive my failure. Ms. Sienna demanded I let her walk the backyard alone. I tried to tell her that I had to stay with her and she refused."

"Tell me what happened," I had to stop from snarling in anger and frustration.

"We can not find her Sir. We have been combing the woods but we cannot find her and her scent vanishes near the garden where we picked up a stranger's scent."

My wolf roared inside of me and I staggered. I moved past the kneeling shifter and out into the backyard. I could smell her light fragrance as I moved towards the fenced garden. When I reached the fenceline and caught the now familiar scent of a strange Alpha, I didn't bother to hold back the growl. This was all my fault. I had been distancing myself from her and leaving her alone more and more. If I had been home, been with her, I could have kept her safe. Now that Cali-Ann had finally talked sense into me it was too late and I had lost her.

I turned to find my pack behind me, most of whom stepped back when I faced them. I locked eyes with Cal, "Call Alex from Lake Tahoe now." He gave one curt nod before heading back to the house.

***

I paced the office waiting for the phone to ring. Every second I was here, I wasn't out looking for Sienna and my wolf was not happy about it. We both wanted to be out hunting for her. I needed to find her and bring her home, and kill the asshole who did this to her. I scrubbed my hands over my face and gave my hair a tug, anything to try to relieve the anxiety I was feeling.

"You need to calm down before he calls," Cal said softly from where he was leaning against the wall of the office, "If you answer the phone with the same energy you are displaying now nothing productive will come of it."

I whirled on him, my voice snapping, "You think I don't know that? Do you know how scared she was of this exact thing happening? I promised her she was safe and I let her down. I should have been here with her."

"But you weren't and you can't change the past. What you can do is calm yourself down so that you can find her."

"What if he hurts her? Or kills her?"

"He won't kill her," Cal said with a shake of his head, "Not while she is pregnant with the pup. That's what he wants."

I dropped into the chair and dragged my hands over my face, "I can't believe I lost her. That I lost another person I care about." I whispered and I could feel the panic clawing at my throat again.

"She isn't lost yet, we will get her back," Cal assured as the phone rang.

I snatched the phone from my desk, stopping when Cal touched my wrist. I looked up at him and nodded, taking a calming breath before answering. "Hello."

"Mr. Preston, this is Alex, you called about Sienna," a deep voice responded.

"I need everything you have about her maker, he's taken her again."

"How the hell did you let that happen?" My wolf growled at his accusation.

"She ditched her body guards, because like all the women in my life she's fucking thick headed." I snapped back. At Cal's look I took a deep breath and leaned back in my chair. "Please, I need to get her back."

After a moment of silence he spoke again, "I'll leave immediately with a few of my men and we will see what we can do to help you. We should be there by nightfall."

Chapter 20

Sienna

I couldn't stifle the groan as I tried to sit up, every stiff muscle protesting. I had to learn to actually lay down when I got tired so I would stop falling asleep in the odd positions. My body wasn't the only thing stopping me from sitting up, there was also a set of thin metal bars that pressed into me when I tried to go higher than all fours. Suddenly everything came rushing back and forced myself to swallow the scream that tried to claw its way up my throat as I realized that I was back in the cursed cage I had woken in nearly two years ago now. The next thing I realized was that while I had been unconscious I had been stripped and was completely naked. I had been so stupid to insist on being left alone, this was my fault.

"I am so glad to see my bitch is awake," Kevin's voice sounded like it had in every one of my nightmares, only this time I was awake. "Aren't you going to thank me for bringing you back home to me?"

"I am going to enjoy Alaric ripping you apart," I growled, refusing to show him the fear that had taken residence in my entire being once again.

His laugh chilled me to my core and I fought not to shiver, "Why would you think he would come looking for you? He sure as hell wasn't there to stop me from taking you was he? When will you understand, no one wants you. No one cares about you. Hell, if it weren't for the fact that you had my pup inside you I wouldn't want you and I wouldn't have wasted my time to come after you. Cheap whores like you are on every street corner." The last sentence was nearly a scream as he tore open the cage door and pulled me out by a fistfull of hair. I came out fighting, trying to force my nails into claws as I raked them across his face.

I couldn't stop the scream this time when he threw me across the room, my back slamming into the corner of a dresser. I rolled to all fours and I tried to scramble to the door but he was too fast, driving his knee into my back, between my shoulder blades. I screamed again this time in pain as he jerked my arms up and back, my shoulders straining. I whimpered as I felt the burning sensation on my skin as if someone was sliding live wires along my flesh. But it wasn't live wires, it was rope that he had threaded gold into. When he had bound me tight enough for the ropes to cut into my skin he stood leaving me on the floor sobbing in as close to a ball as I could get at eight months pregnant.

"I see your time in freedom let you forget your manners. Don't worry I will help you remember them, even if I have to beat them into you." His foot came out of nowhere and connected with the side of my face. The sharp pain to my temple was the last thing I felt before darkness took me over.

***

When I came to again I was on my knees on a cold concrete floor. My shoulders were about six inches from the ground, the lowest the ropes would allow. I could feel the cold metal around my ankles, and another around my neck. I let out a sob as I felt hot tears fall from my eyes, the feeling of hopelessness washing over me. I shook my head and forced myself to stop crying, I would not show this monster any more fear. I clenched my teeth as I worked to lever myself back to sit on my heels, relieving the pressure from my shoulders, I knew from experience that if I had stayed like that much longer they would start to separate from the sockets, this wasn't the first time I had woken up in this position. When I felt the pup kick inside of me I felt my tears start up again, but this time in pure relief. He hadn't killed my baby. I tried to pull at the ropes, straining to comfort the small life inside of me. I knew I had to find a way to get free again and to save us both.

"You know, I planned on letting you spend the rest of your life in comfort, but I just can not allow the level of disrespect you showed me." Kevin's voice floated to me out of the darkness of the basement.

I didn't bother holding in my growl of disgust, "Every mark you leave on me, Alaric and my pack will leave on you tenfold. I will watch as they tear you to shreds and I will bathe in your blood you bastard" I screamed out the last, the only way I had to release my anger. I glared in the direction of his voice, chest heaving.

Again he laughed at my threat, "Don't you get it, they don't give a shit about you. You have been here for over a day now, and not a peep. No one is looking for you. Besides, had he actually cared he would have marked you as a mate when he used you. Oh didn't I think I knew about that? I have been watching you since that little run-in at the store. Besides I know that you only slept with him to try and gain yourself a place in his pack, and he knew it too. He was using you the same way I used you, because he knew that's all you are good for. That's all a whore like you is good far, a quick fuck," He stalked towards me and yanked my head back by my hair. "Well that and as an incubator for my pup. Who knows, maybe I'm wrong and that wanna be Alpha, does care about you. I'll find out when I leave your body on the side of the road after I cut my pup from you." He laughed, letting me go and walking up the stairs, leaving me alone in the basement. When I heard the door at the top of the stairs close I finally let a sob escape my lips. I curled around myself the best I could in my restraints and sobbed out my anger and fear. In that moment I knew I would die in this cold concrete room.

Chapter 21

Alaric

It had been nearly a week since Sienna had gone missing and I was losing my mind. I couldn't sleep, only dozing off for an hour or so at a time. I had completely lost my appetite and only ate when Avianna or Melody shoved food in front of me. My shifters had all been sent out to various packs across the United States looking for any hint of where she had been taken. Those who had stayed close had started to avoid me at all costs. Part of me knew that I was once again destroying my people, but I couldn't bring myself to care, not until I had Sienna home.

"Alaric, you need to sleep." Cali-Ann said softly from the doorway to the dining room, which now resembled more of a war room with maps and lists. She had been one of the few people who hadn't started avoiding me. It seemed to be the opposite actually; she seemed to have decided she had to practically glue herself to my side.

I looked up from the map on the table that I was currently looking at, wondering what we had missed when sending out the convoys to have missed her. "I can't sleep, all I do is lay and stare at the ceiling. When I do manage to doze off I wake up to Sienna's screams echoing in my ears, begging me to save her. I need to find her Cali-Ann"

She walked over and set a hand on my shoulder, "I know you do, and we will find her, but you will be of no help to her if you are falling over from exhaustion when we do. Change, go for a hunt in the woods and then sleep. You will think better after you do that."

I nodded knowing that she was right and still I felt like that was me doing nothing. "Can you call and check in with the troops?"

"Of course, and tomorrow we can start calling the other packs to see if they have noticed anything, and maybe start reaching out to any other packs we have connections with."

When I stood, my legs shook and I could feel the exhaustion wash over me. My vision was graying slightly. I ignored the feeling and headed out toward the back of the house. I stripped down on the back deck, dropping my clothes onto a chair. As I walked down the steps I let go of my control so that as I took the last step I ended on all fours. I quickly left the lush grass of the yard to the rougher ground of the surrounding forest. I let go of my human thoughts and gave into pure animal instincts.

***

The run resulted in only about four hours of uninterrupted sleep in the middle of the backyard where I had collapsed in exhaustion. Groggily I made my way upstairs to pull on clean clothes and splash cold water on my face before joining everyone downstairs. I tried to go straight to the dining room but was interrupted and corralled to the back patio where several tables of food had been put out. My wolf side, still close to the surface from the failed hunt the night before, wanted to ravage the tables of food. My human side felt nauseous at the thought of eating and I didn't think I could keep anything down if I tried.

"You need to eat," Avianna said as she steered me towards one of the tables that sat empty other than a fresh cup of coffee, "Sit and wake up, I will bring you a plate of food."

"I need to get an update," I argued even as I was pushed down into the chair. It was like they knew who to send to make sure I didn't put up a fight. Even in the state I was in, me and my wolf both agreed that we could never hurt Avianna even with our words.

"I will make sure you get a full update boss, but first you need food to keep your energy up for when we get a lead on where Sienna is and we go to bring her home" Cali-Ann said, dropping into the chair across from me two overloaded plates in hand, one of which she set down in front of me. "If you eat your food I will give you an update, but if you stop eating I stop talking."

I wanted to growl at her, to remind her who I was. To remind them all that I am the Alpha and King of this pack, but I couldn't bring myself to muster the energy. Instead I lifted the fork and started in on the pulled pork that had been piled on my plate. My stomach revolted as I ate the tasteless to me food but when Cali-Ann began recounting the phone calls she had made over the last several hours I forced myself to keep eating. Not only had she checked in with the pack members out scouting but she had also reached out to every pack in a three state radius to see if they had encountered any lone shifters. My beast growled when she said that she had informed them all of Sienna's past, wanting to protect the woman who had already gone through so much. Even though I agreed with my wolf, I understood why she did it. They couldn't help us if they didn't know what to look for.

"I didn't reach out to the Alaska packs, I figured you would have more of an in with them than anyone else here." She said, ending her update. As soon I figured I had gotten all of the information from her I put the fork down and stopped eating.

"Thank you." I kept my voice low as I stood and made my way back through the shifters on the porch and into the house. I kept my head down and avoided conversationwith anyone until I could close myself into the office. I took a breath and tried to calm my wolf before I dialed my old friend and Alpha.

"This is Yuma," an old, thickly accented voice answered. Despite the fact that I had been the Alpha of my own pack for over five years I still felt an immediate wave of calm wash over me at the sound of her voice.

"I need your help," And with those four words the entire story fell from my lips starting with when Sienna had knocked on the door.

***

It took over an hour to give Yuma all of the details of the last several months. By the time I finished I was nearly as exhausted as I had been the night before when I had fallen into bed still as a wolf.

"You do seem to find yourself in hard places my friend," Her voice was still calm as always, "I will ask around and send scouts out to the Canadian packs. I am not sure if it will help as that would mean he was able to take her across the border, which is not easy with an unwilling participant. If I learn anything I will call you. In addition I will talk to the spirits to see if they can help you to find your Sienna and ask the spirits to see to her safety."

"Thank you Yuma," I ended the call and let my head drop to the desk.

"What did she say?" Melody asked softly and I looked up to see her standing in the doorway.

"That she would reach out to the Canadian packs and the rest of the packs in Alaska. I feel hopeless Melody. I thought I was protecting her by keeping someone with her and saying away." I felt my chest burn as my eyes began to blur. "I failed her, just like I failed Raylene and Kate" I couldn't hold back the sob. And when Melody rushed forward and wrapped her arms around me I clung to her as my grief poured out of me.

"This isn't your fault Alaric, and you haven't failed her. We will get her back." Melody whispered as she held me.

Chapter 22

Sienna

I tried to ignore the ache in my shoulders and in my calves. I lost track of how long he had left me like this, my arms pulled up and behind my back, forcing me to balance bent over and on my tip toes. I knew it hadn't been too long as the numbness hadn't set it yet. I knew that I could stay like this for over a day before the pressure would start to pull my body apart, this wasn't the first time he had put me into this exact position. So far he had been almost careful of me, making sure not to push my body too far where it would have caused any danger to the baby, but that was the only mercy he had graced me with. Knowing that I new he would be here soon to move me.

My time in this position wasn't the only thing I had lost track of. I had no idea how long I had been here. The only clue I had was that the shift hadn't taken me since I had woken up back in Kevin's tender mercy. Using that I assumed that it hadn't been a month yet, but it had to be getting close. If I was lucky maybe I could use it to get away again. My stomach grumbled and a wave of nausea rolled over me from the hunger I felt, then again if he kept starving me I wouldnt have the energy to run even with the change. I jerked in my chains as I heard the basement door slam open and the sound of footsteps pounding down the stairs.

"How's my Bitch feeling today?" he growled a moment before I heard the metal clang of a bowl hitting the ground.

"Please," I felt something inside me crack as I begged him for the first time since he had taken me from Alaric's estate, tears streaming down my cheeks to land on the concrete beneath me. I knew the bowl meant that he was going to give me some form of sustenance, but I knew that it wouldn't be enough.

He grabbed a fist full of my newly hacked hair and jerked my face up to him, "what was that?"

"Please stop, please just leave me be," I ached for the safety of Alaric's arms, "Please I hurt and I'm hungry. Please just let me go." I sobbed.

"I don't think so," He pulled me up as he loosened the ropes from the ceiling. As soon as my weight bore down on my legs, my knees buckled under me and I fell to a heap at his feet. The only thing keeping my face from hitting the floor was his hand fisted in my barely two inch long hair. He had hacked off what little growth I had early on, even threatening to take a razor to my head, "See you have something of mine and I want it." He crouched behind me and jerked my head to the side, bearing my neck to him. "Maybe if it's a strong healthy pup I'll keep you around to give me more, maybe we'll stop after one more, maybe I'll stop when you die birthing one." he scraped his teeth over my skin, where a mating mark would go and I tried to jerk away with a whimper. "And if not I'll gut you and leave you to rot on the side of the road like the trash you are," he growled into my ear before shoving me forward. He kicked the bowl in front of me and poured in the thick chalky liquid of the protein shakes he has been giving me in place of real food. At the site of it my heart sunk. "Now drink up whore, can't have you starving my child." If he only knew how starved the baby and I were, starved for the safety of Alaric's estate, the pack and my friends.

Forcing back the sobs I shuffled forward on my knees and began to lap and slurp at the liquid, my stomach grumbling again as soon as I smelled it. The moment I was focused on the food substitute, he clipped the chain attached to the wall to the collar that had been a permanent fixture around my neck since I woke up in this hell hole. I was so focused on the excuse for food in front of me that I never saw his foot coming, until it connected with my cheek. I fell over and felt my head bouncing off the floor with a crack before the world went black once again.

***

As I came to again, the first thing I felt was a throbbing in my cheek and another on the opposite side near the top of my skull. I struggled to my knees, the world swimming around me as I did. The struggle was made harder by my arms still fastened behind my back and my progress was stopped when my head collided with the top bars of a cage. I growled, rage racing through my body. I hated this fucking cage. I screamed, the only way I had at the moment to release the anger I felt.

"Well look whose awake," Kevin's voice was like ice water, washing away my rage and turning it to the all too familiar terror, "And who the fuck do you think you are growling and screaming at bitch?" I just looked up at him, feeling all the emotions I was feeling drain away the instant our eyes met. It was then that I knew I was going to die in this basement. I didn't doubt that now, and the knowledge left me numb. The moment I had my baby, he would kill me. I would never see my child, I would never hold them in my arms. I would never see Alaric again, or feel him holding me safe. One day, in the near future, I would be lying dead on this very floor.

"I'm sorry," I murmured, gaze dropping.

"Not yet you're not but you will be. I think you can skip your next meal, and breeding stock doesn't need to see." he sneered. He turned and walked up the stairs flipping the lights off and closing the door.

I shifted until I could lay back down, the cold bars digging into my skin as I curled around my stomach, "I am so sorry little one," I whispered my voice filling with tears. I wasn't sure how much more of this I could handle, how many more meals I could skip. I had moved past hunger and nausea, into numbness. I couldn't feel my hands anymore, and the loss of feeling was slowly creeping up my arms. I finally let go of the small amount of control I had been holding and sobbed into the dark, my hot tears the only thing I could feel. He had finally done it, he had broken me completely.

Chapter 23

Alaric

I looked out over the grounds from the office window, watching as the first snowflakes of the year began to fall. I watched them fall to the ground as hopelessness creeped in a little more every moment I had no word on Sienna. We had expanded our search all the way through Mexico and down all the way to Panama. Every pack in North America was on the lookout for Sienna, and there was still no sign of her. Cali-Ann had even started sending people to check the Bahama's and still there was nothing. We were three days away from the full moon, almost a full month since I had held her, and I itched to run and hunt, to tear my teeth into flesh and feel the hot sweet gush of blood. I yearned to let loose the rage that had been building inside me every day we went with nothing new to go on.

"Alaric?" Cali-Ann's voice was soft from where she stood in the door. I knew that my beast had been mostly in charge for the last week to the point that very few people came near me. Cali-Ann, Cal, and Mark were the only ones to bring me the check-in reports, and Melody and Avianna kept bringing me food. The way things were going I knew that I needed to be away from everyone when the moon took me, I knew that when that happened I would be a danger to anyone around me. I thought about talking to Cal, about taking over the pack and I could start over again and hide away from the world somewhere. I could be the hermit in the mountains somewhere, that way I would only be a danger to myself. If we didn't find Sienna soon it was probably the safest thing I could do for the entire pack.

I dropped my head to the cool glass of the window and waved her in, until I decided to hand over the throne I had to pull myself together and take care of the people I hadn't failed yet. I heard the door close and the lock engage before she spoke again, "talk to me boss." her voice was soft, and close behind me. I looked over my shoulder at her, and I knew from the look on her face that my wolf, my beast was in my eyes. "I have known you for longer than anyone else here, this is not you. You are not mean or cruel, you do not take your anger out on those around you. And yet, since Sienna was taken that is exactly what you have done. What the hell is going on with you? I am not leaving this office until we get this worked out, until I see the leader I know you are standing before me again." I wanted to argue with her, to tell her that she was wrong, but I couldn't. I couldn't argue with the look of mixed confusion, confidence and care in her eyes. I didn't have the energy to even try.

Sighing I scraped my hands over my face and dropped into the desk chair, "I don't know if I can do this again." The words were barely a whisper and I had to fight to keep the tears from forming in my eyes. Ever since the conversation I'd had with Melody I had found myself crying more and more, and I hated it.

"What? What is it that you can't do?" She moved in front of me and sat on the desk.

I looked up at her, letting her see all of the warring emotions in my eyes, "Love someone else."

Her own worried eyes softened, "Oh Alaric, You can't go the rest of your life without love. No one here would hold it against you for finding someone after Raylene."

"I can't love someone again, not like that." I shook my head refusing to meet her eyes.

"Why not? Don't you think that maybe the reason you feel that way is because you already love her? Why do you have be alone Alaric?"

"Because," The word was barely a whisper, but the words stuck in my throat, "everyone I have ever loved died. They all died because I couldn't protect them. I have already failed Sienna, I can't let her die like they did. I have to stay away once we get her back, maybe send her back with Alex."I took a deep breath, "Or maybe she can stay here, I'll leave. I can leave the pack to you and Cal. All of this has to have shown everyone that I'm not the leader they need, I keep tearing everyone apart. Or we can do both, I leave the pack to you and Cal and find Sienna a safe place to stay," Before I could think of another safe place for Sienna my head whipped to the side and my cheek stung. It was so sudden that it took me a minute to process that Cali-Ann had just smacked me across the face. "What the fuck?" I growled glaring at the shifter in front of me, her own eyes now filled with blazing fury.

"I am so done with all of your self loathing crap," she growled, "I have put up with it since you showed up in Bedal. I thought when we merged with the Westerguard clan and you could see how generations could flourish you would get over it, and I think you were. Then we lost Raylene, not just you, but all of us. You don't get to wallow in self pity over it. I get that you lost your family when you became a shifter, but so did most of us from Bedal. But you are right about one thing. If you can't get your head out of your ass, then you should send Sienna away, because she deserves someone who won't run from what they feel. And if you can't step the fuck up and be the leader I know you can be, that Raylene believed you could be, then walk away from the pack. You should be good at walking away by now. You walked away from your family when you changed, you drank yourself away after killing Gordon, and you have been withering away since Raylene died. Sienna is just your latest reason to give up." Before I could respond, she strode from the room, slamming the door closed behind her hard enough to rattle the frames on the walls. I dropped my head back in frustration and closed my eyes, wondering when my life had become such a mess.

***

I jolted awake in the office chair at the pounding on the door. "Come in," I ordered scrubbing at my eyes, forcing the exhaustion away. Mark stepped through the door, and I could feel his anxiety and excitement from across the room. I sat up more alert, "What is it?"

"My King, we think we found them!"

I leapt from the chair, ignoring the way it banged into the wall before falling to the floor with a bang, "Then why the hell are we still standing here?" I followed him out the door, and into the flood of shifters leaving the house. I grabbed my bike from where it had sat since I had first gotten home to find Sienna missing. When I felt the rumble of the engine I knew that my world was finally coming back together.

Chapter 24

Sienna

I shivered in the cage and shifted positions again, trying to find any type of comfort, but everything hurt. I didn't know how long he had left me in the dark cold basement, I didn't think it had been quite a full day. The last time he had come down he had cut the ropes from my arms and I nearly screamed in agony as the blood rushed back into my muscles. Before I had gotten the feeling back in my arms he had forced me to crawl around the basement. He had something with him this time that he would shock me with every time I slowed or tried to stop. It wasn't until my palms and knees were so raw that they were leaving small bloody prints that he finally shoved me back in the cage. Since then he had only given me the crappy protein drinks only a handful of times. By now hunger was just a distant numbness, much like the rest of my pains.

Everything had been numb until I was woken up by a wave of agony. I curled in on myself as another wave of pain washed over me, centering around my stomach. I sobbed and clutched at it. I didn't know what he had done, but deep down I knew that this was it. I was dying. He had finally managed to kill me, and not just me but also my baby. I didn't know what was happening but I knew that my baby was in distress and there was nothing I could do to help them. As the ripples of pain subsided I panted softly. I sobbed, wishing I was back in my room at Westerguard Manor, safe and healthy, not losing the only thing that had given my life meaning in the last year. I wrapped my fingers around the bars of the cage and grit my teeth as another wave of pain washed over me, tightening around my stomach. I fell against the side of the cage when it passed and I contemplated calling out. Kevin may kill me but he would make sure that the baby survived. Before I could make up my mind another wave crashed over me and I lost all breath to even try to call out for help. Over and over again the waves of pain crashed into me like I was standing on the shore of the ocean and a storm was brewing.

I could feel exhaustion creeping in, the bursts of pain from the last few hours sapping what little energy I had left. I shifted and let my head rest on one of my arms, numb to the constant pain of the bottom bars of the cage as they dug into my already bruised skin. I closed my eyes as I stroked a hand over my stomach, sending apologies to the child I hadn't been able to protect. Before I could slip into unconsciousness another crippling pain washed over me, finally ripping a cry of pain from my throat. As it subsided I dropped back down to the floor of the cage, wondering how long the torture would go on before death came.

***

I didn't know how long I dozed in and out, the pain pulling me from the short bits of rest I seemed to be getting between the ripples of pain. It had seemed to have been going on forever and I was starting to wish I could fall asleep and never wake up again. In those moments of consciousness I knew that the embrace of death was the only mercy I would ever have again.

When I heard the sound of the door upstairs slamming open I jerked upright before crumpling from another onset of agony. I heard Kevin yell upstairs and then there was another loud crash. He must have come home in a mood. Ignoring the more constant ripples of pain I tried to push myself back into the corner of the cage, hoping he would find dragging me out to be too much work and would just let me die in peace. I heard an enraged yell from above me and whimpered, terror slowly filling me. If he was so angry he was screaming and breaking his furniture, I knew that I would be next. After several minutes silence fell and then I heard footsteps drawing nearer to the door of the basement. As the door opened I sent up a prayer to any deity that was listening for mercy. When I saw that there were multiple sets of feet coming down the stairs I wondered how much he had charged them all to watch my death. I shuffled in the cage until my back was to them. They may be there to watch my suffering but I didn't need to look them in the face as I died. My fear would not be entertainment for Kevin and his sick, twisted friends.

Chapter 25

Alaric

It took us nearly a full day to make the drive to the address we had. When we finally pulled up the sun was setting behind us. The house we pulled up to was a small ranch style home with two windows on the front on either side of the door. It sat on a street like any other street in any city in the country. I couldn't believe that so much evil had happened in such an ordinary looking place.

I parked my bike directly in front of the small walk that led up to the tiny rickety looking wooden porch. I gave the others a few minutes to park their own bikes and then cars, fanning out along both sides of the street. As I stalked up the walk, my beast just below the surface, I could feel my people falling into step behind me, Cali-Ann on my right, Cal on my left. I pounded twice on the door before stepping back and aiming a kick just to the side of the handle. I heard the wood splinter just before the door swung open, slamming into the wall.

"Who the hell are you?" a voice growled from the left as I stepped into the small run down living room. I wrinkled my nose at the stench that permeated the air like a cloud of pure pollution. The owner of the voice stood maybe five foot six inches and was the first overweight shifter I had ever met. His stomach bulged and drooped over his beltline. The stained shirt stretched to tissue paper thinness across his gut. I was guessing that at one point the shirt was white, but now it was a dingy grayish tan, and his jeans were stained with tattered bottoms and thread bare, thin knees.

I glared at the disgusting slob "Where is she?" I let my wolf out into my voice, and I knew my eyes had shifted color.

"Come for the little whore have you?" he smirked and I watched his hands stretch and reform into claws. "I can't wait to show her your dead, mangled, bloody body."

I hear a chorus of growls behind me. "He's mine, go find Sienna." I ordered as I let my own nails slip into claws. It wasn't something every shifter could do, but a trick I had learned pretty early on. I heard everyone else rush into the house around us like we were an island in the ocean and quickly flooded the sorry excuse of a house. I braced myself and just as I suspected the man launched himself at me. With a flash of speed I backhanded him, much in the same way I assumed he had done to Sienna multiple times, and sent him spinning into the TV and the rickety stand that it was on. Both folded under his weight so he was laying on a crumpled heap of trash "Is that the best you can do? Can't hold your own unless it's against a human woman or a shifter who you treat like a dog until they break to your will?"

"The bitch needed discipline," He growled as he staggered to his feet, wiping blood away from where his lip split.

"You are the only bitch in need of a lesson," I moved across the room and grabbed him by the throat, my claws sinking into his flesh as I lifted him to his feet. I laughed as he dug his own claws into my arm, "I think I will bring her your heart as an apology for break-ing my promise to her." My voice was barely discernible around its growl as I shoved my hand into his stomach and angled up under his rib cage. He coughed and blood bubbled from his lips, his eyes going wide. I wrapped my claws around the beating lump of mus-cle in his chest before ripping it out and let-ting his limp, twitching body fall to the floor. I dropped his heart on his chest as it gave the last few feeble beats, "then again, maybe not." My claws slowly slid back to nails just as

Cali-Ann's voice rang out from farther in the house.

"We found her in the basement, Ric, you need to get down here."

I turned my back on the body on the floor and quickly made my way toward where her voice came from. I hastily made my way into the dark basement and my heart stopped at the sight in front of me. Sienna was huddled around herself in the back of what looked like a large dog cage. Even from the back I could see her ribs and could tell she had lost more weight than was healthy for her, especially as far along as she was in the pregnancy. I took another step towards her and kicked something that skittered across the floor in a clang of metal. I looked down and saw the metal dog bowl and my vision went red. I closed my eyes and calmed myself. I knew that if I tried to help her when I was this angry I would only scare her more. Once my beast calmed again I moved towards the kennel and dropped to my knees. I had to fight not to just rip the door open but instead twisted the padlock until it fell apart and forced patience as I opened the two small latches and swung the door open.

"Sienna, love," I kept my voice soft as I half crawled into the filth covered cage. I reached out and the sound that escaped her was more animal than human. Gently I pulled her out of the cage with me and into my lap, "Someone go get her clothes to wear." Just as the words left my mouth a hot wash of fluid released into my lap. My eyes darted up to Cali-Ann's "and get Cora ready for us, she is having the baby."

Someone came down with a large blanket and we wrapped her in it.When I carried her back up the stairs she burrowed her face in my chest and I was thankful she didn't see what I had done to the man who had taken her from me. As much as I would love for her to see that he died a horrible death and that he would no longer be able to hurt her, I held her tightly and walked out of the door. When I tried to lay her in the back of one of the SUVs she clung to me, unwilling to part. I tossed my keys to one of my pack members for my bike and climbed in with her.

"Get us back to the mansion, immediately!" I ordered as I rocked her gently.

***

We made it back to the mansion in record time and I rushed Sienna into the house, to the small room we had dedicated to Cora for a work space. I laid her on the small bed and brushed a hand over her forehead, assuring her that it was safe to let me go. Just as Cora walked into the room, arms ladened with supplies Sienna arched off the bed and screamed in agony. I watched a calm reserve wash over Cora.

"My King, you need to leave. I am not sure where she is in her labor journey, but I need time to assess Sienna and the pup. I can sense your fear and that will do nothing for her." Before I could argue I was pushed from the room and the door was closed firmly. I stepped back, legs shaking. I couldn't lose her.

***

It had been hours since Cora had pushed me from the room and I couldn't bring myself to leave the hallway outside the door. I could hear Sienna's cries of pain and had to keep myself from forcing my way into the room. I know each woman has a different experience laboring, but what I am hearing sounds like much more pain than when my own children were born. I buried my head in my hands, wondering if there was something wrong or if it was just the fact that this was the first birth I'd heard since my change.

"Alaric," Mel rushed down the hall, Cal close behind her with Aurora in his arms, "how is she?"

"She's having the baby," I looked at the door and shook my head, "her water broke just as we found her, but I dont think it's going well."

"And what about you?" Cal asked.

I looked at the other man, and let the fear show in my eyes. If I had learned anything in the last year it's that if nothing else I could trust these two. "I can't lose her," My voice broke at the words, and when Melody's arms wrapped around me, my knees buckled giving out from under me. I sobbed into her shoulder as the fear of loss washed over me, taking all my defenses with it. "I love her and I can't lose her, I just can't lose anyone else."

"You won't" Mel's voice was soft, "Cora is the best there is and she will do everything to save both Sienna and the baby. She has never lost a pup yet and she won't start now."

"I'm sorry," I pulled away and scrubbed at my face.

"You have no reason to be sorry." Cal clapped a hand on my shoulder giving it a re-assuring squeeze.

***

I jerked awake as the door to the room opened. I wasn't sure how long it had been since I had dozed off leaning against the wall across the hallway. I got up quickly, my heart stopping at the look on Cora's face.

"What's wrong?" I asked moving to the door, not willing to let her push me out again.

She sighed and shook her head, "The pup turned, I can't get them into position. On top of that Sienna has been in active labor for nearly forty eight hours and tonight is the full moon."

"What does that mean?" I ran a hand through my hair and looked past her to where Sienna lay, her face twisted in pain and paler than the last time I saw her. Laying in that small bed, I ached so badly to go to Sienna. I wished I could wrap myself around her, letting her use my strength to get her through this.

"We are out of options. We have to do a C-Section. If she was human they would give her a spinal anesthesia that would numb her from the chest down but there is nothing we can give a shifter that will work for more than a few minutes. We will be cutting her stomach open to save this baby and she will feel every second of us cutting through every layer of her abdomen before we remove that baby. And then we still have to suture her up. She has just suffered nearly a month of torture and starvation, I dont know if she will survive this but it is our only option."

"Have you told her?" my voice was a horse whisper.

"No, I thought it would be better coming from someone she knows, especially someone who can be there to give her a hand to hold through this. I felt my stomach turn but nodded my head and moved past her.

Chapter 26

Sienna

I whimpered and wanted to let death take me. I lost track of time since Alaric had left me on the bed, lost track of how long the pain had been going on. By this time all I could feel was a constant rippling pain. My pelvis felt like it was being ripped in two. The feeling that I need to push is so strong but Cora said I would hurt the baby or myself . I want to push more than I want my next breath.

"Please," I whimpered as Cora softly pushed me back on the bed and ran a cool hand over my forehead.

"I know Sienna, we are almost there." She cooed softly, and her voice grated.

"Hey hun, this isn't gonna feel good, but then we should be good to go ok?" Avianna traded spots with Cora and took my hand in hers. As her words ended I felt hands on my stomach before pain blinded me and I screamed until my breath ran out. I heard murmurs at the end of the bed and then the door opened. As soon as it did I could smell Alaric and felt a calm settle, even over the constant pain.

Cora stopped him in the door and whispered words to him. He went pale for a moment and whispered back. Cora responded and Alaric gave one short nod and moved to take the hand that Avianna wasn't holding.

"Hey Darlin," He brushed his lips over my forehead and I wanted to cling to him, to beg him to make the pain stop. "You have done so well, and it's almost over, but" he looked away and I could tell he didn't want to tell me the rest, "we have to make the pain a little worse.

The baby is stuck, Cora can't get them into position."

"What does that mean?" Fear filled every ounce of me, pushing even the pain further away.

"We have to do a C-Section, but since you are a shifter we can't give you any pain meds for it." Alaric said and I could hear the fear in his voice.

"It will save the baby?" I asked. I knew women died from C-sections but I couldn't remember what the statistics were for the babies.

"Yes." Alaric said, his voice soothing.

"You'll make sure the baby is ok?" his eyes hardened and I knew what he was going to say but I shook my head, "No Alaric, you have to promise you will take care of my baby no matter what happens." I gritted my teeth against the fresh wave of agony, but waited for him to nod his head. It only took a few seconds but felt like hours until he did. "Then do it." I gripped his hand tighter.

"We have to strap you down so you can't move." His voice was soft and as soon as the words left his mouth I felt someone begin to tighten straps around my thighs. I closed my eyes and forced myself to breathe slowly, even as another strap was tightened just over my protruding stomach. Panic at being restrained bubbled up so quickly. I couldn't hold the scream as the blade began to split my skin. When I felt the second pass of the blade the world around me faded to black.

***

The lights were bright as I blinked my eyes. My stomach muscles rippled in pain and I wanted to scream, to beg for the pain to be done.

"Hey, easy there," Alaric's voice swept over me and instantly I calmed. I blindly reached a hand out to him and when his warm rough palm wrapped around my own , he was leaning over me, his green eyes filled with concern. When he pressed his lips to my forehead fear spiked through me. Panic rose like a massive flood. "You shifted over the night with the rest of us and that helped to heal you some, but you still are in pretty bad shape." I could feel the tension in his hand but I couldn't figure out what would have caused it.

It took a moment for my mind to wrap around the fact that I had been unconscious long enough to shift and shift back. "My baby?" Panic spiked through me. That's what he had to be trying to protect me from, what he was trying not to tell me.

"Is fine. She is absolutely gorgeous and healthy. She has all ten fingers and all ten toes. She was 18 inches, 6 pounds 5 ounces." Alaric provided a smile softening his face.

"It's a girl, I have a baby girl?" Suddenly the pain and fear subsided while I considered the news, not fully believing that I am now the mom of a healthy baby girl.

"Once you are a little more stable Cora will bring her in for you." I closed my eyes and sobbed. Every pent up fear released and I clung to Alaric as he wrapped his arms around me.

"You're safe, I'm here and you have nothing else to worry about now." All I wanted at this time was to see and hold my baby girl, but knowing my baby was safe, the pain came back. The severity of the pain had me drifting back to unconsciousness, but in that moment I fought to hold on.

"You have to give her a name."

"We can name her once you are feeling better" he soothed, running a handover my hair.

"No, We have to do that now, Yvonne, it was my grandma's name. Yvonne Marribel Martinez." I whispered trying to fight back the pressing darkness.

"Ok, I will make sure it's taken care of. Now sleep sweetie, you can't take care of her until you are feeling better." He whispered. Hearing his reassurance I let myself sink into the dark again.

***

The next week was hell. For the first several days everything I did hurt. I couldn't sit upright because it put too much pressure on the wound, but laying flat seemed to pull at the healing skin. Alaric hovered like a mother hen to the point I wanted to tell him to go for a run, but a small part of me was terrified to have him leave my side.

The next time I woke up after that first time Alaric was in a chair next to me, a small bundle in his arms. The moment he put her in my arms I felt like everything I had endured over the last two years never mattered. As soon as I saw that tiny baby I knew I would do it all over again for her.

After that I pushed myself to get better, Cora and Alaric both trying to get me to slow down. When Cora finally said that I was healthy enough to travel, Alaric packed Yvonne and me up and took us to his trailer in Bedal. I had never been there but as soon as we stepped inside I knew that this was going to be a new favorite place of mine. While the mansion had everything a girl could dream of, the small trailer provided us the space to be together without interruption. When I saw the nursery in the small spare room my heart soared. After the first night, me and Alaric decided that it was simpler to have Yvonne in the main bedroom with us and I watched, giggling, as he muscled the crib through the narrow hallway. That night, after she had fallen asleep Alaric had tickled me until our laughter woke her up. When Alaric brought her back to the bed with us I finally felt like I was home again.

Chapter 27

Alaric

I sat on the porch of my old trailer and watched as Sienna leaned over Yvonne and kissed the baby's forehead, her newly grown hair forward around her face. Vonnie's squeal of laughter peeled out over the lawn and I couldn't stop the smile that stretched my lips. It had been nearly three months since I rescued and then nearly lost Sienna and Yvonne all in the same day. She had been unconscious for nearly a full day, even sleeping through her change which had terrified me despite Cora's assurance that she was fine. It had taken another day for her to heal enough to stand up and walk short distances. It was a full week until Cora gave her the green light to leave the mansion. As soon as Sienna was given the okay to travel I bundled her and the baby into one of the pack's bulletproof SUVs and took them to the trailer. It had been weird pulling up to my old home but as soon as we stepped inside I could tell by Sienna's face that I had made the right decision. Seeing the smile on her face when she saw the nursery I'd had Cali-Ann set up for me let me know that I never wanted to see any other look on her face.

When I had decided to give Sienna more than a few weeks Cal and Cali-Ann had taken over the day to day running of the pack for me. With Sienna, Vonnie, my nickname for Yvonne, and me joining them only for the larger get togethers, and most of those had happened here at the trailer. I knew that soon I would need to move back into a more active role in the pack, but I wanted to give Sienna as much time as I could to adjust to all of the changes in her life. I figured that the lack of nightly night terrors was a good sign. I set the glass of sweet tea that Sienna had made on the small worn wood table and stood up. I forced myself to walk down the steps instead of jumping over the rail. Sienna was getting better but still tended to flinch when I forgot to move slowly. I let myself fall bonelessly on the new spring grass next to my two girls and brushed a kiss over Sienna's cheek, slipping my arm around her waist.

"How are you two lovely girls doing?"

Sienna's relaxed smile forced my own wider, "we are just fine, though I am thinking someone is ready for a n-a-p."

I rose to my knees and swooped the small baby up letting her bounce a little before settling her in my arms. "Does my little Vonnie need a nap?" The last word had the small baby screwing up her face in preview of the scream she was working up.

"You said the word, now she is yours," Sienna said, shaking her head with a grin. She stood and pressed a kiss to the top of my head before walking back into the house. She had barely reached the porch when the small bundle in my arms began to wail. I quickly stood and cuddled the baby closer, letting my body sway and began to rock her to sleep, the hummed lullaby falling from my lips like an old memory.

***

I looked in on where Sienna had curled up on the bed around the bassinet that Yvonne was asleep in. We had tried moving the crib into our room but it hadn't worked as well as I remember from my first set of babies. After about a week I had sent Cali-Ann out shopping for one of the new bassinets that sat right on the bed. Once we had that we all slept better at night.

I still didn't know what I had done to have earned not only a second but now a third chance at a happily ever after, but I was not about to question it anymore. Closing the door I sent out a quick text for Melody and Cal to head out to the trailer. Walking out to the living room I sighed. It had rained that morning so we had been inside all day and it showed. While I waited for them to arrive I picked up around the trailer, unable to sit still, afraid that my nerves would get the better of me. It had been so long since I had lived with a baby and had forgotten how much stuff they came with, and I swore there was more now than the last time I'd done this. It didn't help that everytime Sienna showed me anything baby related I immediately forwarded it to Cali-Ann to pick up for us.

I just finished putting all the bins filled with baby toys and supplies back on their shelves when I heard the car pull up outside. I took a quick inventory to make sure we were low on anything before I grabbed my jacket and keys from by the door and slipped outside, closing the door quietly behind me. Between the rain that morning and the setting sun, the warmth from the day before had cooled significantly.

"Is everything ok?" Mel rushed from the car, meeting me at the bottom of the stairs.

"Everything is perfect. Sienna and Vonnie are asleep but I don't trust leaving them alone, at least not unprotected." I looked at them. "I need to run a few errands, would you be willing to stay here with them until I get back?"

"Yeah, we can do that." Melody said as Cal walked back to the car and pulled Aurora from where she was asleep in her car seat. Melody studied me, her head tilting to the side as if she was trying to solve a puzzle. "Are you sure everything is ok Ric?"

I pulled her into a one armed hug and dropped a kiss to her forehead, "It will be. I will be back by lunch tomorrow, if Sienna asks just say something came up with the pack."

"What are you planning?"

"You'll see." I grinned and swung myself onto my bike.

***

The ride into Seattle seemed to take forever and yet no time at all. It had been awhile since I had ridden the bike and it felt good to feel the air on my face again. I wondered if I could get Sienna on the bike with me one of these weekends. I stayed the night at the pack headquarters, though sleeping without Sienna next to me was harder than I had expected, and spent the next morning checking on a few things I knew I had been ignoring. Once I knew the stores would be open I headed back out on the bike and made my way to downtown. I weaved through the downtown traffic until I got to the mall and then to the small family owned jewelry store behind it. I parked toward the back of the full lot and jogged into the building. The jewelry store at one corner had only a handful of people milling around the glass cases, pointing at the glittery jewels below. I joined them and let my eyes pass over the dozens of rings covered with small jewels and overly large centerpieces. None of them were anything that I could ever see Sienna wearing. I had nearly given up hope when my gaze caught on a small heart shaped diamond set in silver with a small band lined with tiny diamonds as a wedding band.

"Can I help you Sir?" I looked up to see a middle aged woman in a navy blue suit on the other side of the counter.

"I need one of these in a size eight please."

"Are you sure Sir? We can offer you something larger and have several payment plan options if you need." I looked up and saw the look of distaste in the woman's eyes.

I let my eyes go hard and cold. I was used to people underestimating me in my scuffed boots and worn leather jacket, but that didn't mean it didn't still piss me off. I pulled out my wallet and slapped several crisp hundred dollar bills on the glass counter, "a size eight in that exact ring." I let just the edge of a growl fill my voice. I watched her eyes go wide and she nodded before scurrying away to the back room. It took only another twenty minutes and I was on my way back to the trailer.

Chapter 28

Sienna

I smiled down at the giggling baby on the changing table, my giggling baby. I pressed a kiss to each tiny foot before pulling socks over them. I still struggled a little getting her legs into the small stretchy pants but I had just gotten them pulled on over her diapered butt when Alaric stepped up behind me. I smiled over my shoulder at him as he pulled me back against him, arms wrapping around my waist. It still surprised me how easily we fit together when we stood like this.

"Are you just about ready to go?" He laid his cheek on the top of my head.

"I am, though I wish you would tell me what this is about." I lifted Vonnie into my arms and cuddled her to me as I snuggled back into Alaric, letting myself sink into the safe feeling he gave me.

"All I know is that Melody and Avianna are on their way to kidnap and pamper you."

"I would rather stay here with you and my baby girl," I cooed the last words down at the little girl dressed in pink, "especially since you were gone almost all day yesterday."

"I told you, I needed to handle some pack business that I have been ignoring. Now you need to go so that me and this little munchkin can get some more one on one bonding time," he reached around me and slipped the baby from my arms and stepped away from me. It left me feeling cold. "And you can get a little mommy time."

"Are you trying to get rid of me?" I turned to look at him, sliding my arms around his waist. I tried to ignore the feeling of abandonment that suddenly filled me, like he was trying to push me out. I tried to tune out the small voice in the back of my head that was whispering now that I'd had my baby that was all Alric had wanted me for, and he wanted me gone for good.

"No, but I don't want you to overwork yourself. Newborns aren't easy work, and you didn't exactly have an easy pregnancy or birth. I want you to go and relax and when you get back, me and you can go out for dinner. I am sure Aurora would love a playdate with Yvonne." He shifted the baby up onto his shoulder more before he pulled me into him and pressed his lips to mine. The kiss was long and deep and warmed me to my core, washing away all the doubt that had been there just a moment before. I lifted myself up so I could try to deepen the kiss more, wanting to feel more of him, my mind flashing back to our one night together. Yvonne's gurgles pulled me back to the present and I let my forehead drop to his chest, panting softly.

"Hello, we are here." Avianna's voice called out from the living room. Alaric chuckled softly above me and I felt my cheeks flush red.

"Come on, it's time for you to head out," He slid his arm around my shoulders and we all made our way out to the living room. "And how are my other two favorite girls?" he asked as we joined the two ladies in the living room.

"Don't let Cali-Ann hear that she isn't in your top three," Melody grinned, "Though I'm sure we could set up a pretty good betting pool when she kicks your ass for even implying it." When he laughed I couldn't stop myself from grinning up at him.

"So will you two tell me where we are going?" I asked as I stepped into my boots and pulled on my leather jacket that Alaric had brought home for me after his trip the other day.

"It's a surprise,"Avianna smiled as she grabbed my hand and pulled me out of the door with her.

***

The drive took us to the nicer side of Seattle, and Cali-Ann was leaning against the wall of the store we pulled up in front of. Just from the outside of the building I knew that this was a place I never could have afforded on my own.

"What is this?" I asked as we climbed from the car.

"Mommy Spa day," Cali-Ann grinned.

"We all thought you could use a little pampering after everything, and Alaric seemed to agree." Avianna's voice was quiet as she stepped up next to me.

I felt my eyes fill with tears as I looked at the three girls that stood around me, my new friends. My new family, "I don't know how to thank you all." I couldn't help the sob that escaped as they all hugged me at once.

"None of that now, we are here to relax and have fun," Avianna said, reaching out to brush the tears from my cheeks.

"And you can thank us by coming inside, allowing yourself to be pampered ten ways to Sunday next to us while we all charge this to Alaric's personal credit card," Cali-Ann grinned holding up the thin bit of plastic. We all laughed and I wiped the last of my tears before following her inside.

They had made appointments for the full treatment for all of us. We were led to a small private locker room where we each stripped down to nothing and wrapped ourselves in the softest robes I had ever felt before. I rubbed my face into the collar of it and grinned as I cuddled into the knee length robe.

"You know if you want one I'm sure we can bring one home with us," Melody said softly from where she was stepping into a pair of sandals.

I smiled up at her, "I may just have to do that. This is probably the softest thing I have ever worn."

"Are we ready ladies?" a voice called through the door. We all grinned like school girls at each other before filing out of the room.

***

I couldn't hold in the groan of pleasure as the masseuse dragged the heated rocks over my muscles before kneading her fingers into my tense flesh. I could hear the others making similar noises from where they were getting the same treatments. I had stopped trying to keep my eyes open within the first few minutes of the massage, instead sinking into the feeling of deep relaxation the fingers along my back induced. When the heat and pressure stopped I couldn't bring myself to try to even open my eyes again, instead choosing to lay limply over the padded table.

"You ladies take your time and when you are ready we will take you out to the next step of your treatment." our guide's soft voice said before the door closed.

"Do we really have to get up?" Cali-Ann whined from where she laid on her own table.

"Do you want the pedicure?" Melody asked before pushing herself up with a groan of effort.

"Damn, you do make a good argument." Cali-Ann grumbled.

Despite the fact that it was an effort to sit up I was smiling as I did. "Come on girls, onto the next stage of pampering." I encouraged cheerfully.

***

When we stepped out of the spa nearly three hours later every single one of my nails gleamed a light gold, I had a dusting of make-up that was barely there while still highlight-ing every one of the features I never knew I had, and my hair had been trimmed, curled and styled so it brushed along my cheekbones yet never obstructed my view.

"OK you guys, why did you insist on the makeup and hair do?" I asked as all four of us slid into Melody's SUV.

"Alaric asked us to spoil you so he could take you out tonight." Avianna said from the back seat. "So we are going to take you shopping for an amazing dress and matching shoes."

"You guys don't have to do that."

"Girl, you are not taking away my chance to spend my King's money," Cali-Ann laughed from behind me.

"We are enjoying ourselves," Melody assured me, "and we wanted to do this. Avianna said it, you haven't had an easy couple of years and you deserve this." With her reassurance I let myself relax back into the seat.

***

When we finally made it back to the trailer that Alaric had moved us to shortly after Yvonne's birth I was wearing the new outfit that the girls had nearly bullied me into. They had picked out a gold silk sheath dress that hugged all of my curves, yet still hid the remainder of my mommy tummy. The neck draped just low enough to hint at cleavage and the bottom of the skirt flared ever so slightly around my knees allowing me to walk easily even in the low heeled shoes they had insisted on, because they were the same color of the dress according to Avianna.

Alaric was waiting on the porch when the car stopped. I took a moment to take in the dark suit pants and light tan dress shirt he had on and when I got out of the SUV I enjoyed the way his eyes widened when he saw me. "You are absolutely stunning." He greeted coming down to meet me at the bottom of the stairs.

I couldn't stop the blush that blazed across my cheeks and dropped my gaze from his, "Thank you."

"Ready for dinner?"

My eyes shot back up to his, "What about Vonnie?"

"Vonnie is my problem tonight," Melody said from next to me, "I think Aurora and her will have a wonderful little playdate and you two can get a full night's sleep."

"Are you sure?"

She smiled warmly at me, "I am positive. You two go and have an amazing dinner." Taking her at her word, Alaric slipped an arm around my waist and guided me to his own

SUV. He held the door open, giving me a hand into the higher vehicle before making his way to the drivers side and getting behind the wheel. As we pulled out of the driveway he took my hand in his and pressed a light kiss to my knuckles before letting our entwined hands fall to rest on the center console.

Chapter 29

Alaric

Sienna had taken my breath away when I saw her get out of Melody's SUV. Even as we made our way toward the city I had a hard time keeping my eyes off of her, especially when the setting sun would glint off the material of the dress she wore. I had to keep my breathing slow so as to not show her how nervous I was, knowing it would spook her.

"Are you sure everything is ok?" She asked again, looking over at me, eyes filled with worry when I met them.

I smiled back, doing my best to make it a relaxed and reassuring smile. "Everything is fine.

You are gorgeous." I gave her hand in mine a light squeeze before letting my thumb brush back and forth over her knuckles the rest of the drive.

***

When we got to the restaurant I asked Sienna to wait for me to come around and open her door. After helping her down I slid my arm around her waist pulling her into my side as we walked to the restaurant. Again I held the door for her and walked in after quickly falling into step with her, not wanting to be far from her side tonight.

"Hello, I have a reservation under Preston." I said to the older gentleman behind the podium just inside the door. I watched as his eyes roved down over the list infront of him.

"Ah yes, I have you down for a table for two Mr. Preston," he smiled up at us, "If you would like to follow me we have the table ready."

Sienna looked up at me, "Why are we some place so fancy?" she whispered suspiciously.

I just grinned down at her, "Because you deserve to be wined and dined." I kissed her softly, just a brush of lips knowing that Cali-Ann would kill me if I ruined the professional make up before the end of the night. "Just enjoy it darling." When she narrowed her eyes at me I just smiled wider and kissed her again, deepening it just a little hoping to distract her. The table we were led to was a small round table draped in white with a single white candle just off center toward the back of the table. I pulled out one of the chairs for Sienna and waited for her to sit before moving around to the other side of the table. I laughed softly when I saw her eyes widen as she looked over the menu. "Order what you want, anything you want." I said reaching over to give her hand a squeeze. When the waitress came by I ordered us a bottle of wine and smiled when Sienna added an order of the spinach and artichoke dip appetizer. When she came back with the open bottle of wine we both ordered our meals, both opting for the steak, one of the shifter staple foods.

"Did you have fun with the girls today?" I asked after the waitress walked away with our order and I poured us each a glass of the off white transparent liquid.

She smiled back over the table at me, "I did. I don't think I have ever had a spa day before coming to this pack. It was a lot of fun, even more than when Melody had someone come to the house shortly after I got here. I think though that the best part was having friends to spend the time with, it was way better than doing it alone."

"I'm glad you are finding your people here Sienna," I squeezed her hand softly again, wanting to assure her that I meant every word. We continued the small talk until the food arrived and then I ate while watching Sienna. I loved that every feeling she had was expressed on her face again, that she had stopped guarding her thoughts so hard from everyone around her. When the waitress brought out the chocolate souffle I had pre-ordered, her eyes went wide in delight and I knew I had made the right choice. She ate about half of the small chocolate dish before she pushed it away and looked up at me.

"I can't eat another bite."

I grinned, "I take it you enjoyed it?"

"It was amazing, all of this has been amazing." she smiled, "Thank You."

"You are very welcome. You deserve amazing Sienna." I slipped the waitress my card when they stopped again and soon we were on our way back out of the restaurant. When the door closed behind us I looked down at Sienna, "I know it's getting chilly and that they put you in heels, but can I talk you into a short walk around the park over there?"

Sienna curled a little tighter into my side, her arm tightening around my waist. "I think we could manage that." I smiled and wrapped my arm around her shoulders, letting my hand rub along her bare arm to keep her warm. I led us down the path until we stood near the fountain that had only just been turned back on from its time off over the winter. When we stopped in front of it she let her head fall against me, and I felt her body relax.

"Sienna," I said her name softly, not wanting to startle her.

"Hmm?" was the only reply I got. I smiled down at her and pressed a kiss to the top of her head before stepping away just enough to turn her to face me. She looked up at me, her large brown eyes filled with nothing but trust that had my breath stopping in my throat.

"I need to get this out. When you knocked on my door all those months ago I was drowning in grief and I never thought I would feel anything but pain again. Then I lost you, and I realized that I had started to feel again, I had started to feel for you. When I finally had you in my arms again I was told that I might lose you still. But now I have you, and I have Yvonne. I never want to lose either of you ever again." I let myself fall to one knee in front of her. The cold concrete through my dress slacks barely registering to me as I pulled the small black velvet box from my pocket where it had been all night. "Sienna, I want to be with you for the rest of our lives, I want to wake up next to you every morning, and I want to spend every weekend building forts in the living room with you and Vonnie. So, will you make my dreams come true and marry me?"

I held my breath as she looked down at me, her lips parted, her eyes wider than I had ever seen them before. It wasn't until she nodded her head, tears slipping down her cheeks that I could breathe again. I pulled the ring from its velvet encasement and slid it onto her finger. As soon as it was in place I stood and pulled her into my arms, kissing her as deep as I could. My beast growled inside me at the soft mewls she made. Pushing down my own needs I pulled back and rested my forehead against hers.

"I have one more question for you, will you let me claim you as my mate? Tonight?"

"Yes, now please." were the only words that she said as she pushed herself against me and fastened her mouth back to mine.

I grinned back, "How about we go get a room and do that somewhere more comfortable?"

She grinned back, "probably a better idea."
***

I drove us to the first nice hotel I saw and tossed the keys to the valet even as I pulled Sienna from the car and rushed both of us into the lobby. I guided us to the front desk and waited for the clerk to look up at me.

"Hi, how can I help you Sir?"

"I need a suite for the night please," I said, sliding my credit card and I.D. across the desk.

"Let me see what we have Sir," she smiled as she took both cards and moved to scroll through her computer. It took a few moments and she looked back up, "We do have a penthouse suite available for the night."

"I'll take it," I said not wanting her to say the amount knowing it would make Sienna uncomfortable.

She nodded and began tapping on her keyboard while looking at both my I.D. and my credit card. She turned on her chair and grabbed several sheets of paper from the printer behind her. Turning back she slid two room cards through the little swiper on the desk. Then she slid all of it back to me, "Please sign here and here." she said making two small X's.

I quickly signed the two lines and grabbed all four cards. "Thank you" I grinned at her before we turned to nearly run to the elevators. We separated when we got inside the small box but I had to fight the urge not to shove her against the wall and take her there. I slid one of the room cards into the slot on the elevator and hit the button for the top floor. The ride up those fifteen floors was the longest I had ever taken. I stood back to let her out of the elevator when the doors opened directly into the room and counted to five before I followed her. As soon as I stepped in the room she was in my arms, plastering her body to mine.

I reached down to slide my hands up her legs, sliding her dress up as I did until I could grip her thighs and lift her. She wrapped her legs around my waist and her arms around my neck as she sealed her mouth to mine. I carried her to the bed and crawled onto it with her still wrapped around me. I sat back on my heels sitting her on my lap so I could pull the silk dress from her. As soon as it fell to the bed her hands were pulling at my own shirt, forcing it up and over my head. Once the fabric was out of the way our mouths fastened to each other again.

"Need you now," she whined into my mouth and I laid her back, pulling away just enough to push my pants off as she kicked her panties down her legs. Moving forward I gritted my teeth as I slowly entered her, not wanting to hurt her. When I was fully inside her wet heat, she moved her legs back around me and the heels of her shoes dug into my lower back as I began to slowly work myself in and out of her. I ran a hand up her body until I could wrap my hand into the black silky strands of her hair and gently I urged her head to tilt, for her to bare her throat to me. I peppered kisses and nips along the exposed skin as I worked her closer and closer to her release. Only when I heard her gasp my name over and over as if on repeat, and her nails dug into my back, did I sink my teeth into that vulnerable soft spot of her neck, claiming her as my mate. Then I let myself empty inside of her.

Chapter 30

Sienna

I stared at myself in the mirror. The white silk was bright against my dark skin. The bodice held the sweetheart neckline tight to my chest, pushing the mounds of my breasts up. It was tight around my waist until my hips where the silk draped to the floor. There was a single slit up the center of the skirt to my knees that allowed easy movement and the train trailed out about four feet behind me. My dark hair had been piled high with only a few curls left to fall loose around my face and brushed along the tops of my shoulders. I had opted out of a veil but the others had talked me into wearing one of the pack's tiaras. It was a simple silver band lined with diamonds. It was the only jewelry I wore and it glittered atop my head where it sat fastened to my ebony hair.

"You are gorgeous." Melody said from next to me.

I met her kind gaze in the mirror, "I'm scared."

Avianna joined us at the mirror and they both hugged me from either side, "What are you afraid of?" They both were wearing burgundy colored silk dresses, the tops were similar cuts to my own, but the skirts ended just a little past their knees.

"That this is all a dream. I have an amazing soon to be husband. I have a beautiful baby. Amazing best friends, more friends than I have ever had before." I slid my arms around both of them hugging them tighter, "I don't know how I ever got this lucky but it all feels like a dream."

Melody kissed my cheek, "just wait until Alaric is in one of his snits and we throw you to the wolf, literally." She grinned, "Then I want you to remember that this is a dream." We all laughed and I had to brush away the tears before they could fall.

"I think it's time girls." Avianna said with a smile. I followed them out of the small room and down the hallway to the back of the mansion's property. As Melody opened the door the music began. Avianna gave me one last smile before she followed Melody outside. I waited until I heard the music change and both doors were pulled open before I stepped out into the bright sunshine. My breath stopped in my chest when I saw Alaric at the end of the aisle. Next to him Cali-Ann stood in a dress similar to Melody and Aviannas but in black and white instead of the deep wine color of theirs. When I caught my breath I made my way toward him, the world seeming to slow around me and my eyes never leaving his bright green ones. When he took my hands, time seemed to snap back into place with a rush. The pack officiator started the ceremony, but I quickly tuned him out, losing myself in Alaric's gaze.

When the officiant said my name, I was pulled from my haze and turned to look at the shifter standing between and behind us.

"Sienna," he said my name again, "Do you have vows to read?"

I took a deep breath and nodded. I looked up at Alaric and dropped all of my shields, "Alaric, when I first came to you I was broken and scared. I never expected to find love here, I never expected to find a family here. But I did. You protected me when I needed it, even when I didn't want it. You forced me to see myself as you saw me, beautiful and whole. I know you were in your own dark place when we met but I can only hope that I have provided you with as much healing and love as you have given me. I love you with every beat of my heart and I promise it to you from now until it's last beat." I heard several sniffles from the crowd and from behind me but it was the glisten of tears in Alaric's eyes that had me blinking back my own.

"My King?" the officiate urged softly.

"Sienna, You say that I saved you but you brought me back to life. The day you knocked on my door I was ready to give up. I was living only to fulfill a promise, not for myself. The first time I saw you though, afraid to so much as meet my eyes I felt a renewed sense of purpose. A purpose that grew even as I fought myself. I told myself that I was no good for you, but in truth, I can't live without you. You and Yvonne are my entire reason for living and I will do everything in my power to protect you and keep you both with me."

The officiant barely had time to get the final words of the ceremony out before I was in Alaric's arms and his mouth was fastened to mine. All around us was the sound of cheers and when we pulled apart I couldn't stop grinning.

***

I laughed as I watched Alaric spinning a giggling Aurora around the dance floor.

"It's so good to see you smiling." Avianna said, settling into the chair next to me, "and to hear you laugh."

"It feels amazing to finally have so many things to smile and laugh about." I reached over and took her hand in mine, giving it a squeeze, "Thank you for being such a good friend."

"You are very welcome," she smiled and leaned over giving me a hug.

"Think I can steal her for a dance?" Ryan asked from in front of us, a hand extended out to Avianna.

"Go," I said, giving her a soft shove. I only had a few moments to watch them before Alaric was in front of me tugging me to my feet. I laughed as he spun me out onto the dance floor, pulling me back into his arms just as the music slowed.

"You are gorgeous," He whispered softly.

"You cleaned up pretty good yourself," I smiled as I cuddled in against him while we swayed softly to the music. I tilted my head up at him, "What would I have to barter for you to leave that tux on when we get to the hotel?" I asked, wiggling my eyebrows.

He laughed and ducked his head down to brush his lips over mine, "I think that can be arranged Mrs. Preston,"

I grinned wider, "I like the sound of that."

Epilogue

Alaric

I sat back down in the sun-warmed wooden rocking chair, the small baby boy snoozing softly against my chest now that he had on a fresh diaper. The trailer in Bedal has become a vacation spot of sorts as traveling with little ones was exhausting. Being King and Queen also hadn't left us much down time for traveling the world. I smiled as I watched Yvonne and Kai running through the back yard.

"How is the newest member of the family?" Sienna asked, settling herself into my lap.

"Much happier now that he is dry. And how is Momma?" I asked pulling her down for a gentle kiss.

"Happy," She smiled as she reached out to run a gentle hand over the small baby's head. "Thinking it is maybe time to head back to the castle soon." I rolled my eyes at Sienna's nickname for the pack's mansion. It had taken her a little time to get used to being in the role of Queen but with Avianna and Melody by her side she had begun to thrive.

"Are you sure? It's barely been a month, we can take more time for you to recover and adjust to a third baby."

"I'm positive." she smiled, "Honestly a third hasn't seemed to be as bad as adding the second. Besides, I think everyone is excited to meet their newest little prince. Avianna has been asking to see little Declan for the last three days."

"If you are sure then we can pack tonight after the kids are down and head back in the morning," I said, giving her a squeeze around the wait, "I love you."

"I love you too," she leaned in and kissed me softly and everything in my world was right. The way it had been ever since the first time I held this woman in my arms all those years ago.

***

We got back to the estate late the next day and I could see the remnants of a cookout.

"Looks like we owe Kai for that meltdown this morning," I smiled over at Sienna.

"You know this is only pushing off the inevitable." She laughed as we began to pull the sleeping toddlers from the car. I was just pulling Declan's car seat from the car when the front door opened to reveal a heavily pregnant Avianna.

"You should be asleep," I said as we walked past her into the house.

"I wanted to see the baby," she whined before following me to peer into the carseat, "he's so small and adorable." she cooed.

"Just wait until yours is here and waking you up at all hours." Sienna said from next to us.

"Here let me take that." Avianna said moving to grab the diaper bag from her friend.

"I got it, you need to go get off your feet, you are due any day now." she said, turning her body.

"Speaking of," I said, setting the carseat down on the small bench and setting a hand on Avianna's shoulder, "After the baby is born why don't you and Ryan go to the trailer for a little bit. it's a good place to decompress and bond with a new little one."

"Really?" she nearly squealed.

"Of course."

"Thank you," just then there was the sound of liquid on hardwood and I saw the small Omegas eyes go wide, "I think my water just broke."

***

It took nearly two days but eventually Avianna and Ryan added a gorgeous little girl to the mix. I was brought to tears when they told me that they were naming her in Raylene's memory and had given her the name Raelynn. Though I wasn't sure who was more excited to see the new babies, Melody or Aurora. The little girl who had brought the only smiles to my face before Sienna came into my life had grown from a beautiful baby into a gorgeous little girl. As the last several years had passed I watched as she quickly befriended Yvonne and they had formed a bond much like Raylene and Melody had had when I first met them. The only thing she was better at than being a friend was a big sister, a discovery that we made when about six months after Kai was born Melody gave birth to a little boy that they had named Liam. Now it was Avianna and Ryans turn to add to the group and in that moment I realized that while I had lost my family to that attack so many years ago, I had made myself a new one.

About Author

Ana Michelle was raised in Southeastern Wis-consin, with two

younger siblings. Reading books was the best way to get through the winters

there. Ana started writing in the sixth grade as her escape during summer

vacations. Since the first time she sat down with a computer to type her first

story, her aspiration was to be a writer. Garnet Fire is her debut novel and

the first book in the Gemstone Witch Series.